W9-BNH-849

Dear Reader,

What if the behavior of the quantum world overtook that of the macro world? That's the question William Sleator asks here, and his answer provides one of the strangest, most addictive sci-fi experiences of recent years.

This is science so boggling it *should* be fiction—particles that leak through seemingly impenetrable barriers; a photon that travels through two holes at once; a particle that is only real because it is observed. The quantum world breaks the rules of the larger world we live in.

When Susan and Gary, a teenage sister and brother living in gothic isolation, notice bizarre events taking place in the vast gardens around their home, they quickly become caught up in a world where nothing is predictable and every choice leads them farther and farther from home. This is William Sleator at his classic sci-fi best, taking theory and giving it diabolical life in a story that shakes our perceptions of the world, micro and macro.

Good luck in the maze,

Susan Van Metre
Senior Editor
Amulet Books

Other books by William Sleator

Novels
Blackbriar
House of Stairs
Into the Dream
The Green Futures of Tycho
Fingers
Interstellar Pig
Singularity
The Boy Who Reversed Himself
The Duplicate
Strange Attractors
The Spirit House
Others See Us
Dangerous Wishes
The Night the Heads Came
The Beasties
The Boxes
Rewind
Boltzmon!
Marco's Millions
Parasite Pig
The Boy Who Couldn't Die

Books for Younger Readers
The Angry Moon
Among the Dolls
Once, Said Darlene

That's Silly

THE LAST
Universe

William Sleator

Amulet Books
New York

With thanks to Lily Weiner, who advised me on
instant messaging style.
—W. S.

Library of Congress Cataloging-in-Publication Data:
TK
ISBN 0-8109-5858-9

Published by Amulet Books
a division of Harry N. Abrams, Inc.
100 Fifth Avenue
New York, NY 10011
www.abramsbooks.com

For my sister
Lucy Victoria Sleator Wald
1946–2003

THE LAST UNIVERSE

FOREWORD

"If quantum mechanics has not profoundly shocked you, you haven't understood it yet."

—Niels Bohr, Nobel Prize–winning physicist

Einstein hated it. No one wanted to believe in it, even those who discovered it. But they had no choice. Quantum mechanics is true—though the Nobel-winning physicist Richard Feynman said that nobody really understands it.

Quantum mechanics describes the behavior of matter at its tiniest levels—atoms, protons, electrons. Our whole world is made up of them, yet their behavior is completely different from the way things work at our level, and frighteningly counterintuitive to us. Here, you can kick a ball and see where it goes and if you have the right equipment you can measure how fast it's going. We can measure and predict the movements of planets and meteors and asteroids. But in the quantum world you can't. Heisenberg's Uncertainty Principle states that if you know how fast an electron is going, you can't know where it is. In fact, it doesn't even have a definite position; it is in more than one place at the same time. The most you can know is the probability of finding it at a certain location. Uncertainty is everywhere.

Schrödinger, one of the founders of quantum mechanics, was so bothered by this idea that he devised a famous thought experient called Schrödinger's Cat to show how absurd quantum mechanics is. You imagine a cat in a box. Also in the box is a vial of poison and an electron. If the electron hits the vial, the poison is released and the cat dies. If the elctron does not hit the vial, the cat lives. Since initially the electron is in two places at once, the inescapable conclusion is that the car is both dead and alive at the same time. As bizarre as this seems, no one has been able to show that it can't actually happen.

Another interpretation is to say that there are two universes, one in which the cat lives and one in which it dies. And now it has been scientifically demonstrated that in fact there really *are* an infinite number of universes, created by tiny changes at the quantum level that create bifurcations in the universe. There is no way we can get to any of them.

But in science fiction you *can*. In *The Last Universe* I have taken these real principles of quantum mechanics—uncertainty, unpredictability, a cat that is dead and alive, and infinite universes—and applied them to a family's parklike garden and a maze, in this world, not the quantum world. The garden and the maze begin to behave in very peculiar—and frightening—ways. And there is no way to stop it.

—William Sleator

u wont bleev what i overheard valerie say 2 jen," Lisa's message was appearing in the instant message box. "i hardly ever go 2 the mall, but i was in the bookstore and they were in the next aisle, where the fashion magazines r. they didn't see me. valerie sd she was worried about u, nobody ever saw u any more, and"

There was a knock on the door of my room. I groaned. It could only mean one thing. I ignored the knock and just kept reading.

"—and jen sd . . . well, maybe I better not say . . ."

"what did she say?" I wanted to know, typing fast.

The knock came again. "Susan," Mom said. "Gary wants to go to the garden. He hasn't been out all day."

"Okay, I'll be right there," I said to Mom, feeling a little bit frantic.

"they never wld have had this conversation if they knew i could hear," Lisa's message was appearing. She was avoiding my question.

"what did jen say?" I asked Lisa again.

"o . . . she sd u were acting funny 4 awhile."

I sighed. But I wasn't surprised, knowing what Valerie and Jen were like.

"and I found the coolest book. its all about how"

"sry, g2g," I wrote back. "gary wnts 2 go out."

"u don't want to hear about my new book?"

I could almost hear the hurt in Lisa's voice, and she was practically the only friend I had left. But what could I do? "i hv 2 tk hm out 2 the grdn, now. hes sick. he cnt walk," I wrote.

"y dont they get sombdy else 2 tk cr of hm?" Lisa wanted to know. "y duz it alwyz have 2 b u?"

"its like, they thnk its my duty," I wrote. "and he wants me 2, for some reason. and how can I rgu when hes sick?"

"Susan, please," Mom said, as she pushed open the door.

"by, lisa," I wrote. "ttyl. pos. sry. cya." I logged off without waiting for her to reply, hoping she would forgive me.

I turned around. Mom was looking sadly at me. "I

know it's hard on you, too, Susan. But think of Gary."

"Okay, okay, sorry, I'm coming now," I said, standing up. At fourteen, I was taller than Mom; I was one of the tallest girls in my class. In one way it was a drag to be taller than most of the boys my age. In another way it was good to look older—because older boys were beginning to notice me. It was summer now, school had just gotten out, but I was already looking forward to high school next year, and the older guys. *And when I am back at school I won't have to spend so much time wheeling Gary around*, I thought, then felt guilty.

I followed Mom down the stairs. "And . . . and be pleasant to him, too," Mom said softly, as if Gary might hear us. "Try to make it fun for him. It's important. You don't know what it feels like to be . . . to be . . ." She took a deep breath. "To be going through what he is," she managed to say. In a minute she'd be crying.

"Okay, we'll have fun," I said. "I'll go right now." I wanted to get away before she broke into tears.

Gary was in his wheelchair in the kitchen, which is at the back of the house. He must have hated that wheelchair so much more than I did—he'd been in it for almost a month now. He'd been a great athlete, as well as a good student, good at everything—track, swimming, football—and now he was stuck in this chair. I never knew what to expect from him these days.

"The weather looks pretty good but it could change any minute," he said impatiently. "Come on, let's go."

I stifled my response to being ordered around by him. I knew he hated needing me.

Dad was proud of the plywood ramp he'd built over the short flight of steps from the back door, even though he was sad the whole time he was doing it, because of what it meant about Gary. If we didn't have this ramp, Gary wouldn't be able to go out at all. And now that he couldn't walk, Gary's favorite thing in the world was going out.

Out into the garden. The garden I'd always hated, and stayed out of as much as possible. But now, with Gary like this, I couldn't avoid it like before. It wasn't just the difficulty of pushing him around in the wheelchair over the uneven ground. It was the garden itself that was the disturbing part—the garden, and Gary, too.

If I wasn't so tall, I wouldn't have had to do this so much. But Mom had much more trouble with the wheelchair than I did. And what I had told Lisa was true. They all wanted *me* to be the one to wheel Gary around—especially Gary. He was sixteen, two years older than me, and before he got sick he hadn't wanted to spend any time with me at all. He'd always been doing sports, and at home he'd mostly ignored me, poring over his science books—he loved science. Now he wanted me to wheel him around as much as possible.

Was he punishing me?

I propped open the back door and took hold of the two rubber hand grips on the wheelchair. The ramp wasn't steep: Dad had made the slope as gentle as possible so it would be easy to negotiate, but the wheelchair still pulled me down it. I was always scared of losing control. I had to take small steps, pulling back on the handles as I went so slowly down. Every time, I wondered what would happen if I just let go of the chair.

Dad had inherited the property, which had been in his family for generations. That was why the garden was so big—land around here had been cheap when his great-grandparents had bought it. It had been farmland then, not the suburbs, but no one in the family had been a farmer who grew crops for money. Dad's great-grandparents had inherited some money and invested it in this land. Great-Uncle Arthur, who had also lived in the house, had been a scientist who won the Lebon Prize for quantum physics, for something about quantum mechanics. I had no idea what that meant. Everyone else in Dad's family had been businessmen. All of them, including Great-Uncle Arthur, the quantum scientist, loved to garden, for the pleasure of it, to create something they thought was beautiful.

Dad was an only child, and so the entire place had come to him. Neither he nor Mom cared much about gardening, but they had held onto the property for sentimental reasons; Dad knew that's what his parents— especially his father, whom he still seemed to miss— would have wanted. It wasn't just our ancestral home, it had been a kind of spiritual home to the family for generations, and Mom and Dad knew that. We wouldn't have been able to afford the taxes on all that land, except that Dad was an important real estate lawyer and knew how to wangle things downtown.

Still, before Gary got sick, Mom and Dad had started talking tentatively about selling a lot of the land; the garden was too big to keep up properly, and they could make a huge amount of money from it, and pay for college—for me, at least. Gary would have gotten sports scholarships. Both Dad's parents were dead now and would never have known. I had been so thrilled at the thought of people clearing the land, getting rid of the eerie old glades and rustling banks of shrubbery, and putting up neat houses with clean, open lawns. It would have been so great to have neighbors nearby.

But then Gary got sick, and suddenly he loved the garden so much. It was odd, because when he was well he hadn't cared all that much about it. He had never been afraid of it, the way I was, and he had enjoyed walking around in it, and playing hide and seek and war games with his friends when he was younger. Still, it had never been all *that* important to him.

But now that he was sick, the garden had become the center of his life.

Outside the back door was the lawn that surrounded our old two-story log house. Great-Uncle Arthur, one of Dad's more eccentric relatives, had removed the wooden siding to expose the original huge dark logs with mortar in between them. Even from here, the most open place, you couldn't see another house. The closest one was a half mile away, and Dad's family had made sure to plant thick borders of trees and dense shrubbery all around the perimeter of our land, so that we would have privacy and protection no matter what happened on the property next to ours. It had been smart of them—if you cared about stuff like that—to guess that the land around here would eventually get developed and wouldn't just stay open farmland forever. Apparently most people at that time didn't have as much foresight, and didn't imagine that this area would become a suburb of the city, full of houses with small yards, and malls and traffic.

But because they had planned so carefully, the ten acres behind our house felt completely secluded, especially the large section that bordered on the state park, which could never be developed. It would have been like being in the wilderness, except for the garden. Now that there were no more avid gardeners in the family, it was getting wilder and wilder. It was extravagant of Mom and Dad not to sell the land—a lot of developers wanted it. It was also extravagant of them to hire Luke, to do as much as one person could to take care of it, which wasn't a whole lot, since the garden was so big. But now that it was so important to Gary, they had no choice but to hold onto it.

"Which way do you want to go today?" I asked Gary, feeling apprehensive. It was up to him; he was the invalid. He could decide to go someplace ordinary, or someplace scary. I had noticed over the years that Gary, like me, had avoided the more eerie, distant parts next to the state park. Now he didn't seem to know the difference between what was scary and what wasn't, and wouldn't admit that he ever had.

"The pond," he said, looking straight ahead, almost as though he were talking to himself. "On a day like this, I want to go to the pond."

I hated the pond. The pond itself was small, and surrounded by tall, dense trees. Sun never seemed to go in there, and the water was always dark and gloomy.

Dad's aunt had drowned in the pond when she was five years old. If that hadn't happened, and she had grown up and had her own family, the property would have been divided up, and our part would be a lot smaller. But my grandfather's younger sister had drowned, and the whole place had gone to him, and Great-Uncle Arthur, a bachelor. Then to Dad. I hated to think of that little girl going into the water and being pulled down, crying for help, and the pond so remote that no one could hear her. They didn't find her body for a whole day.

I had the feeling that the drowning wasn't the only bad thing that had happened in the garden. But Dad and Mom were closedmouthed about anything else. We only knew about the aunt because of the old family pictures of her—it would have been impossible for them not to tell us what had happened to her.

"But it's not sunny today. Don't you want to go to someplace brighter?" I asked Gary, trying not to sound like I was begging.

"I feel like the pond," Gary said lightly, ignoring the pleading in my voice. And I knew that if I didn't take him there, he'd complain to Mom and Dad, and then I'd be in trouble. In trouble with my parents, and with Gary, too, and I didn't know which was worse.

I had never been a very assertive person. I usually did what other people, like the friends I used to hang out with, wanted to do. I preferred that to arguing.

I sighed, and began pushing the chair toward the path that led into the group of apple trees on the right. There were only about a dozen apple trees, but we had always called it the orchard. In the spring, the trees overflowed with white blossoms. Now the blossoms had fallen off and were brown and withering under the trees. The sun came out briefly from behind a cloud, and the bright green new leaves shimmered in the breeze, making dappled dancing shadows on the ground as I pushed the wheelchair underneath them. And even though I hated entering this place, I could also feel how the apple trees might be beckoning, enticing.

"The apples from these trees are always the best," Gary said. "Better than any you can buy. Remember climbing up and picking them, Suze?"

I didn't remember Gary and I ever climbing the apple trees. Maybe he had done it with his friends, but not with me. I also didn't like the direction his words were taking, reminiscing about when he could walk, and climb. It could put him in a bad mood.

"They almost make me look forward to the fall, those apples," Gary said softly.

I pushed the wheelchair as quickly as I could over the grass, to get away from the apple trees. Mom and Dad didn't talk to me about what was wrong with Gary, but for several months he had been getting thin and weak, and now he couldn't walk. I didn't want him thinking about the fall and wondering if he'd see it. How could I distract him?

"Those apples are hard and bitter and have worms in them," I said. And then I didn't have to think of a way to distract him. I stopped the wheelchair suddenly. "Look at that!" I bent over so he could see me pointing, my heart thudding. "Those flowers around the outhouse!"

The wooden outhouse and the stone gardener's shed were past the orchard and to the left. The outhouse sat proudly behind the shed, on a slope of land that must have been man-made, it was so steep and abrupt in this flat place; stone steps were embedded in the grassy slope going up to it. Outhouses can be disgusting, but this one wasn't; it was neatly and solidly built, and always clean, with a bucket of lye and a dipper to sprinkle down the hole when you were done, so it never smelled bad. Not that I ever used it, or had even gone inside it in years.

Luke lived in the stone shed below it, which was full of tools, and he was the only one who used the outhouse. Luke was from someplace in Cambodia, some little town I could never remember the name of, where everybody probably had outhouses instead of real bathrooms anyway, so using the outhouse wouldn't matter to him.

Today, for the first time in my memory, brilliant red flowers on tall, two-foot-high stalks stood all around the outhouse. They had grown overnight.

"Don't be a dope," Gary said. "There's always been lots of stuff growing around the outhouse, because of what's underneath it."

"If I'm such a dope then I must be too stupid to find my way to the pond," I couldn't keep from saying. The sky was darker than before now. I gave a sharp tug on the wheelchair and Gary slipped forward slightly.

"You'll do what I want, Suze," he said, and smiled engagingly up at me, as if he wasn't scared by what I had just done. I knew he could tell Mom and Dad if I did anything mean to him; he knew I was in immediate control.

Hinges squeaked and Luke stepped out of the stone shed, carrying a shovel and rake, a trowel sticking out of the pocket of his overalls. His orange cat, Sro-dee, was perched on his shoulder. "Hello, Gary. Hello, Susan," Luke said. He was shorter than me, too, with dark skin, and black hair that fell over his forehead. When he smiled—he was always smiling—his dark eyes turned to slits.

"Those red flowers around the outhouse," I said to

Luke. "They weren't there yesterday. How did they grow so fast?"

Luke turned and looked at them and shook his head, puzzled. "Same flowers we have in my home, in the tropics," he said. "Never think they can grow here."

"Well, but did you plant them?" I pressed him. "Do they normally grow overnight?"

He shrugged. "I never plant them. Maybe the seeds fall out of my clothes or my shoes. Maybe they come from inside my body when I first came here and finally grow up from underneath. A mystery. And I think I know everything about this garden." He shook his head. "Well, I got work to do. Going to rain soon." He turned and walked away to the left, past the little hill with the outhouse on it, disappearing behind it.

I was mad at Gary for calling me a dope, and for ordering me around. It had felt good to shake the wheelchair.

"Please. Can we go to the pond before it rains?" Gary said.

I liked it that he was begging me. Maybe I didn't have to be afraid of what he would tell Mom and Dad. When we were alone together, I could do what I wanted.

My emotions about Gary changed from minute to minute. I resented him, I was often angry at him (though I had always avoided getting angry at people directly). But a lot of times I felt sorry for him, too.

I knew there were motorized wheelchairs; I'd seen people in them on the street. But of course they were much more expensive than this one, which the health insurance had provided. And Mom and Dad probably didn't think it was safe for Gary to be riding around all by himself. That left me to be the one to take him around most of the time. Great. It would have been different if he'd been friendlier to me before he got sick. But we'd never really been friends. And now he was my job.

I pushed the chair past the stone shed and to the right. Here there were banks of shrubs as tall as me, still in bloom, big round white and pale blue blossoms. Tall, scraggly weeds grew up among them now.

The raindrops started to fall when we were halfway down the row of shrubs, and then came a crack of thunder.

"No pond today, I guess," I said, feeling relieved not to have to go there—and also guiltily glad that Gary wasn't going to get what he wanted. "Have to hurry back before we get drenched."

Gary smiled up at me, looking handsome, like in the old days. "Rain won't kill us," he said.

"You think Mom would like it if I let you get soaked?" I asked him.

He couldn't argue about that. I turned the wheelchair around and pushed it back as quickly as I could, which wasn't very fast because it was so heavy and hard to steer, and the ground was so rough and uneven I had to keep pulling it back and turning it slightly and then pushing it forward again. Soon I was panting, and my arms were aching. Back past the row of shrubs, then the stone shed and underneath the apple trees, the wheelchair rocking, and across the lawn toward the dark old log house. I grunted with effort as I maneuvered it up the ramp.

And as I was struggling, Gary said, "We've got to get to the pond as soon as possible. Something's going to happen there and I want to be there when it does."

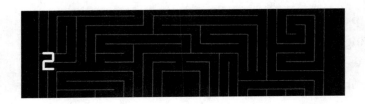

2

Gary didn't sit in the wheelchair at supper. Dad and I had to lift him out of it and slide him onto a regular dining room chair. It had been almost impossible at first. Gary had resisted; he wanted to do it himself and he had fallen down and then refused to eat. After a week he had finally given in, and by now we had the hang of it. Also, it seemed to me that Gary might be lighter now. I didn't say anything about that to Dad or Mom—I didn't want to make them more upset than they already were.

Before Gary got sick, we hadn't usually eaten together. Gary and I would eat whenever we got home. But now Mom and Dad had decided it was important for us all to sit at the table together. I could understand why they felt this way. It created a pretense of normalcy, like a happy family on TV or in the movies. But it would have been so much easier to just let Gary stay in the wheelchair and give him a tray.

The pill organizer beside Gary's plate, which had compartments holding big pills to be eaten three times a day, for every day of the week, wasn't normal at all. But his medication was all important. They didn't tell me things, but I sensed that the pills were keeping him alive.

"Well, I hope you two went out today before it rained," Dad said, as Mom brought out the macaroni and cheese. It was Gary's favorite food and we had it at least twice a week. I was getting really sick of it—all the fat and carbohydrates. Luckily I was growing too fast to worry about getting fat.

"Yeah, just before it rained," Gary said. "But we didn't have much time." He didn't look at me as he said it, but it was clear he was blaming me for not taking him out earlier.

"Why not?" Dad said, looking at me, not smiling.

"She was on the computer for hours," Mom said.

Dad sighed.

I looked down, feeling guilty. Okay, Mom doted on Gary. But there had always been a special bond between Dad and me. He seemed to understand me, and often took my side when Mom or Gary was mad at me.

I hated disappointing him now. Gary, too. They were secretive about what was wrong with Gary, and what his chances were, but it was obvious that it was a life-or-death situation. He was my brother—he had been there for my whole life, and that meant something to me, no matter what.

I looked up, meeting Dad's eyes. "It's just that now that school is out, and nobody ever comes over here anymore, I miss my friends. And . . . I'm sort of stuck here."

"But you need to make compromises. You can talk to your friends when the weather's bad. When it's good—well, you know what's more important."

I felt really ashamed. "I will," I said to Dad, and then turned to Gary. "We'll go out early tomorrow," I said, pretending to sound enthusiastic.

"Whatever," he said coolly. He must have hated Mom and Dad giving me orders about him—it would make him feel weaker than he already was.

"We were out long enough to see something strange," I said, to get away from this subject. "There were these big red flowers all around the outhouse, that grew overnight. I don't remember ever seeing anything like that before. Gary said things were always growing there, but I've never seen anything like these things. Luke said they were flowers from the tropics that never grow here. He said he didn't plant them. You've been here your whole life, Dad. Did you ever see anything like that before?"

He glanced at Mom. "No . . . uh, red flowers around the outhouse? Never."

"I wonder what it means," I said. I wouldn't normally have been that interested, except now I had to spend more time than ever in the garden—and the garden had always made me uncomfortable.

"Seeds blow in the wind," Dad said, serving himself salad. "Unexpected things pop up in that garden sometimes." He shrugged. "And who knows? Maybe Luke did plant them, and wouldn't admit it because he wanted it to be a surprise."

Dad was being evasive. He always was about the garden. He knew I didn't like the place, and now that I was forced to hang out in it he *still* wouldn't answer my questions.

"You never tell us anything about the garden," I dared to say now. "Your Aunt Caroline drowning— that's all you've ever told us."

He and Mom exchanged a glance; he might just as well have said, *There are other things we haven't told you.* But what he actually said was, "This is no time to be morbid, Susan. The garden is an incredible place and we're incredibly lucky to have it. There's nothing else like it anywhere. Enjoy it, use it. That's why we're making sacrifices to keep it. I expect you both to be out there often this summer."

I didn't like the lecture. But it was reassuring that he didn't worry about what might happen to us in the garden. Maybe that meant it wasn't really dangerous after all.

"u shdnt let ur rents boss u around so much," Lisa said in her IM that evening. "ur letting them treat u like a baby. u cant be a baby 4ever."

I tried to get Lisa to understand. "dont u feel sorry for gary at all?" I wrote to her. "ever since he got sick, and especially since he got the wheelchair, all his friends stopped coming. nobody comes here. im all he has and he might not have much time left."

"nobody ever comes there? thats terrible," Lisa wrote.

She said it was terrible, but she wasn't offering to come either. She had never been to the house—we hadn't become friends until recently, and with Gary sick, all visits had stopped. "well i do feel sorry for him" I wrote. "and now im going to go watch tv with him. cya. ttyl."

As I logged off, I wondered what she would do if I just invited her to come here. Since Gary got sick, I had never thought of actually *inviting* one of my friends.

But Mom and Dad were right. Despite everything, Gary was more important than my friends. I went down to watch a science fiction show on TV with the rest of the family. And when Gary said he was thirsty, I hopped up and got him a Coke.

Gary slept downstairs now, in the screened porch on the other side of the house from the kitchen; the porch overlooked the wooded valley with the pink and blue phlox. Mom and Dad and I had moved out the porch furniture and put in a bed and all Gary's other stuff. At night on the porch you could hear the insect noises very clearly—it was about as close to sleeping outdoors as you could get without actually camping, and that's what Gary wanted.

Dad and I helped him into bed, early—he got tired easily these days.

"Tomorrow we'll go to the garden first thing, if it's not rainy," I said to him.

"To the pond, okay?" he said sleepily, looking around at the screens, though with the bed light on you couldn't really see outside.

"To the pond," I said, and Dad and I went back inside.

When the door was closed, Dad looked puzzled. "Is that where he likes to go? The pond?"

"Yeah," I said. "And—it kind of creeps me out, Dad. Mainly because . . . because of Great-Aunt Caroline."

"Funny," Dad said, and cleared his throat uncomfortably. "You'd think he'd want to go to places that were wide open, full of light."

"Yeah, you would," I said. And now I was scared all over again. Dad didn't seem to like the pond either.

It was bright and sunny the next morning. Right after breakfast I worked the wheelchair down the ramp and we set off for the pond.

Gary had decided to be pleasant. "You're getting really good with this chair," he told me. "It's much smoother than it was at first. You're learning fast."

"Oh. Thanks." I was about to say it probably wasn't easy to have to be stuck in this thing, but I stopped myself in time.

It was a good thing he was in this mood, because it took a lot of work to get to the pond. First through the orchard, then past the stone shed and the outhouse which seemed to have more abundant brilliant red flowers than before. I didn't comment on this, because Gary had argued with me about the flowers yesterday, and I didn't want to spoil his good mood. Then the long avenue with tall, pastel flowering shrubs on both sides, where we'd had to turn back yesterday. At the end of the avenue, on the right, we skirted the edge of the valley that went all the way back to the screened porch. Luckily for me, the valley didn't seem to interest Gary—it would have been almost impossibly hard to get the wheelchair down there and especially back up again.

At the edge of the valley, we turned left into the sunlit meadow of wildflowers. There were so many little flowers here in the spring and early summer that you didn't have to worry about stepping on them. Like everything else in the garden, they were pale pastel colors, faint pinks and blues. That was what was so jarring about the new flowers around the outhouse— nothing else in the garden had ever had such an intense color. And nothing else had ever grown so fast.

I liked the meadow—it was about the only part of the garden I did like—but now, with the wheelchair, it was difficult here because the earth sloped slightly upward. Soon I was breathing heavily. But pushing the wheelchair didn't seem as difficult as the last time we had been here. And I had an odd thought: Gary getting weaker was making me stronger.

You could go several ways from the meadow—to the greenhouse to the left, to the rose garden even farther to the left—but to get to the pond you headed to the right, toward the pine woods at least fifty yards away.

There was one path cut through the otherwise impassible woods, only one, and it led from this empty spot in the meadow to the pond.

As the tall trees loomed closer, I began to feel the usual dread. I thought about asking Gary if he was sure he really wanted to go to the pond. But what would be the point? I knew he wanted to go there; he had said it plenty of times already.

It was a sudden change from the bright sunlight of the meadow to the cool darkness under the trees. In one way it was lucky for me that it was a pine woods, because the dead pine needles on the ground kept underbrush from growing, which would have made it harder to push the wheelchair along the path. But no underbrush didn't mean there weren't rustling noises. And the trees on either side of the path were so dense that you could only see a few yards into the darkness. I didn't like that. I knew it was dumb of me, and that there were no wild animals here, but I still couldn't help thinking that at any moment something could come running toward us.

Gary leaned back in the wheelchair and breathed a deep sigh of pleasure. "Isn't it great in here?" he said. "So cool and quiet. We always loved playing in these woods, jumping out and scaring each other." He laughed quietly.

I was glad I had never been included in those frightening games. Just being in here was uncomfortable enough. I didn't need crazy boys to make me afraid that something might attack at any minute. And the path to the pond went on and on. With the chair it would take almost twenty minutes to get there—twenty minutes of pushing.

The halfway point was the rough wooden bridge over the stream. You could hear the water from a distance as you approached it. The stream came from the state park—otherwise it might have dried up by now because of people cutting down trees and laying down pavement in the subdivisions. If the stream had come from another direction and dried up, the pond might have dried up, too. I knew it was horrible of me, and non-ecological and politically incorrect, but there was a part of me that wished that had happened.

It got darker the deeper you went into the trees. The path turned to the right, where the trees were taller and there was even less light coming through. It was silent, except for the rustling of the branches and the occasional birdcalls. We could have been a million miles away from everybody else in the world. Why had that five-year-old girl come all the way in here by herself? No wonder no one had heard her if she cried for help.

Ahead the path widened and I knew we were almost

there. But you couldn't even see the black water until you were just a few feet away from it. That was one of the eeriest things about the pond. You'd think, because of the break in the trees over the water, that it would be lighter here. But somehow the trees contrived to bend together above the pond, so that no more sunlight came through here than in the rest of the pine woods.

And I always looked at the water as little as possible.

What had Gary meant yesterday about something happening at the pond? How could he know, anyway? It had to be just his imagination. But I still couldn't help asking, "What do you think is going to happen here? How do you know?" as I stopped the wheelchair among the ferns at the edge of the water, staring down at the ferns and not at the pond.

"Look" was all Gary said.

I dragged my eyes toward the water.

It was full of plants that had never been there before. Big, flat, round leaves floated on the surface, with vertical edges evenly going an inch up, and from the middle of each group of leaves sprouted a bright purple flower, the color so intense the flowers almost seemed to glow in the gloom. The blossoms were made up of petals about six inches long, flaring upward and outward, and the center of each blossom was a luminous yellow.

"Like the outhouse," I murmured, feeling a little sick. "These were never here before, never. Are you going to tell me this isn't strange, like you did about the outhouse?"

Gary leaned his head back and looked up at me, grinning. "I was just teasing about the flowers at the outhouse. I know they're part of what's happening—just like these are part of what's happening. The quantum garden. The entanglement woods."

"What do you mean? What's happening?" He was scaring me more than kids jumping out from behind the trees. Did he have some special insight, because of his illness? But that was fantastic. I'd never heard of that happening to people when they got sick.

"The garden . . . It's finally doing what they meant it to do, when they started it all those years and years ago." He sounded very pleased with himself.

I felt like crying in frustration—and fear. "Gary! Why are you saying things like this? I don't know what you're talking about."

"I . . . I don't really know either," he admitted, his voice hushed. "It's just this feeling I have—ever since this happened to me. It's a good thing Mom and Dad never sold the garden, I know that now. Otherwise there wouldn't have been time for this quantum thing to happen—whatever it is."

He was scaring me even more. Especially because his personality was so different in here—his hushed voice, his odd predictions about quantum, whatever that was.

"Okay. You saw the pond. Can we go now?" I almost begged him.

"But it feels so good here. There's life in the water going into those lotus flowers. I can feel them making me stronger." He paused. "And if you could pick one and I could bring it back, and put it in a vase on my porch, it would make me even stronger."

"*No!*" I shouted. He wanted me to go into the pond? To put my feet in that black water, where the little girl had drowned? If something had pulled her down, maybe it would pull me down, too.

"Please, Suze," he said, smiling sweetly at me. "It would mean so much. It might . . . help to make me get better."

I groaned. How could he put me in this position? He knew how much I hated the pond.

"And I'll tell Mom and Dad how great you were today. I'll tell them you need time to go and see your friends."

That was an incentive. But entering the pond still seemed unthinkable.

"See how close to the bank that first lotus is?" Gary said. "You'd just have to put one foot in the water, lean forward, and pick the flower. It would take a second.

Then we can leave."

"How do you know that's what they are—lotuses?" I asked, delaying.

"I've seen pictures of them. They're another tropical plan, that never grows in this climate. An exotic. They won't even be here when we're not here observing them. Come on, Susan," he coaxed me. "You can do it, I know you can. For me. And also to earn some extra freedom. Just slip off a shoe and put one foot in and pick it. Only a second and it would mean so much. Please? It would be the best thing you could do for me."

Why was he doing this to me? It was torture. Because as terrified of the pond as I was, I knew he was right. It would only take a second, and my fear was irrational anyway. And he was so sick, so sick. Even though it was unspoken, we all knew he was probably going to die. And I couldn't give him a flower he wanted so much?

Especially since it was so odd of him to want something like a flower. He had always cared about tough-guy things—sports and rough games and hard science. Never flowers.

"Please, Susan," he said in his new soft, husky voice. "I'll never forget it."

What could I do? What choice did I have?

And what would he say to Mom and Dad about me, what would he put me through, if I didn't do it?

I was actually trembling as I bent over and took off my left sneaker. Horrified as I was, I did remember to fix the catch on the wheelchair, so it couldn't roll forward into the pond. I walked toward the water, my heart thudding. I tried to reach for the closest blossom from the bank, but I just couldn't. Holding my breath, I put my left foot into the water.

It was colder than I had expected. I felt for the bottom with my foot, leaning forward. When the water was up to my ankle, I touched the bottom, horribly squishy and muddy. I pulled my foot back, overcome by disgust. But I had gone this far, and nothing had happened yet. I touched the bottom again and leaned forward. I was just close enough to grasp the lower part of the thick stem of the closest lotus blossom. I gave it a sharp tug.

It was strong, and resisted. I pulled at it again, twisting it. It finally began to come loose.

And just as it did, there was a scream from above us. I screamed, too, and jerked, and slipped and fell into the water.

I was scrambling out in half a second, still holding onto the lotus blossom. My top and shorts, hands and knees were wet and muddy. But I was out of the pond.

And I had the blossom Gary wanted.

"What was that? That scream?" I said, gasping, my voice shrill with hysteria.

Gary was laughing. "A crow," he managed to say. "Just a little old crow. Wow, did it ever spook you." And he laughed again.

I was furious. I'd done this really difficult thing to satisfy his whim, and now he was laughing at me for being scared. It wasn't fair. "Here's your stupid flower!" I said, and threw it into his lap. I fumbled my shoe onto my foot and tied it with shaking fingers. I undid the catch on the wheelchair and turned it abruptly and started back along the path in the pine woods as fast as I could go.

"Susan! I'm sorry! Okay? I shouldn't have laughed. But you're going too fast. It's really bumpy. Slow down. Please slow down."

I had never pushed the chair so fast before. It had to be the adrenaline from how scared I was, the fight-or-flight reaction. And I loved hearing the fear in his voice. I went faster. We bumped over the little wooden bridge in no time.

"Please, please, slow down!" Gary begged me. He was gripping the arms of the wheelchair, trying to sit bolt upright but unable to keep from swaying back and forth. "I could fall out!"

I ignored him. Now I could see the bright light where the trees ended. I had to get to the meadow as soon as possible. I needed to be in open space. The light grew closer and closer, brighter and bigger. I was running with the chair now.

We burst out of the trees.

And ran right into a rosebush.

I stopped abruptly. "Huh?" I said. "What are we doing *here*?" We were in the rose garden, which wasn't possible. The path should have brought us back to the meadow.

I pulled the chair away from the bush. It had scratched both of us.

Gary was looking around curiously, not speaking.

"What's happening?" I said, frightened. "This is weird."

Gary clutched the lotus blossom. "You panicked. You went the wrong way."

"I don't know what you're talking about. There's only one path through the woods and it doesn't start at the rose garden." I looked around, trying to get my bearings. We were in the rose garden all right. To the left, on the other side of the rosebushes, I could see the meadow. We were several hundred yards away from where we had entered the pine woods, on this same path, only a little over half an hour ago.

The rose garden hadn't moved. The path to the pond had moved. It was exactly the kind of thing that happened in bad dreams. Only this wasn't a dream.

And Gary wasn't buying it. A few minutes ago he had said something was happening to the garden. Quantum. Entanglement. Now he was saying I was just panicking. Why was he doing this to me?

But I knew I was right. The path had moved.

"We're getting out of here," I said. "This is too much." I pushed the chair around the rosebush and to the left toward the meadow. I prayed that the meadow would still lead to the edge of the valley, and then to the long avenue of flowering shrubs, and the stone shed and outhouse, and the orchard, and the lawn, and finally the house. I prayed that the path to the pond was the only thing that had moved.

Because if anything else had changed, we might not be able to get back home.

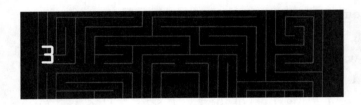

3

I **was out of breath**, trembling, terrified that at any minute something else would end up in the wrong place. I pushed the wheelchair slowly, carefully.

"Funny. I can feel your hands are shaking," Gary said calmly, in his normal voice. "And when we started out this morning, I thought you'd gotten so much better at handling this thing."

He was his old teasing, sarcastic self again. He had been so different in the woods and at the pond, almost in a trance.

But he was still clutching the lotus blossom.

"Why are you shaking? What are you afraid of anyway?" he asked me.

I didn't need this. I stopped again. We were almost out of the rose garden. This place still seemed to be the way I remembered it. "You *know* there's only one path in the woods, and it doesn't start at the rose garden. The path moved. I don't know why that doesn't scare *you*."

"How can a path move?" Gary said derisively, and although I couldn't see his face I could bet he was rolling his eyes.

"What about the outhouse and the pond? How can there be flowers where there were never flowers before? Flowers that don't grow in this climate?"

"You heard what Dad said. Seeds blow in the wind. That's how flowers propagate. It happens all the time."

"You said the lotuses were only there when we were looking at them."

"I did?" he said, sounding confused.

I pushed the chair past the last rosebush. The old greenhouse, with its stone foundation and rusting metal rods holding the curving glass panels in place, was only a few yards away, right where it should be. That was a relief. But Gary's behavior was making me more scared—and angry. "You said it yourself. You said the garden is changing. Dad's family had planned some-thing strange from the beginning, and it took all this time for it to happen, and now it is."

"Funny. I don't remember saying that. Your imagina-tion's getting really vivid these days. Must be a reaction to stress."

I wanted to scream. But I knew there was no point in continuing this conversation with him in this mood. I began to push the chair past the greenhouse, hoping to find the meadow on the other side, and across the meadow the edge of the valley, and everything else where it was supposed to be.

"I feel like going to the greenhouse," Gary said.

Some relative of Dad's had gone to a lot of trouble to make it a miniature version of a large Victorian building in England called the Crystal Palace, and the panes of glass were all rounded in what struck me as an unnatural and ominous way. It was like a fragile glass soap bubble that could shatter dangerously at any moment, damp and musty and falling apart. Some of the panes of glass had cracked and fallen down onto the tile floor in shards and splinters, and there was nothing growing in it anyway but weeds, since Luke didn't have time to keep it up along with everything else. Hardly anybody ever went inside it, and I sure wasn't ready to go someplace else I didn't like today. "I don't feel like going there," I said.

"But I do. And I'm the one who's sick," Gary said. It was the first time he had admitted being sick—to me, anyway. And ever since we had left the woods, he was being more ornery than usual. He was punishing me all right, especially the way he had made me walk into the pond—and fall down—to get him his precious lotus blossom.

And that gave me the perfect excuse. "Don't you want to get your *flower* into water as soon as possible?" I asked him, emphasizing the word "flower" to make it sound a little ridiculous. "You said it would make you stronger, so I don't think you want it to wilt, do you?"

"I said that? I said it would make me stronger?" he murmured, looking down at the big purple blossom in his hands. And he actually sounded puzzled. Maybe he really *didn't* remember what he'd said in the woods; maybe he wasn't just doing it to torment me.

I started pushing the wheelchair away from the greenhouse, taking advantage of his confusion. "You don't remember? That's why you made me go into the pond and pick it for you." The meadow was still normal as we rocked across the pale wildflowers. It took a lot of strength in my shoulders and forearms. My muscles were aching now. I wanted to go and see the place where the path to the pond normally started, but it was not on a direct route to the house and I didn't want to push Gary all the way there. But I had to know.

"Gee, I guess I *must* have made you pick this," he mused. "I know you would never go into the pond on your own."

What was the matter with him? He had seemed in a sort of trance in the woods, then gloating when we got out, and now he didn't remember any of it. And it wasn't just because he was sick; he had been sick for weeks and weeks and he had never behaved like this before.

"Do . . . do you remember the path moving?" I asked him, as a sort of test.

"I remember you panicking and taking the wrong way back from the pond," he said, sounding completely sure of himself about this.

"Well, I'm about to find out about that," I said. "I'll be right back."

"Wait . . . don't . . . ," Gary said.

But I was already running. It felt wonderful to be free of the chair and to just let my legs pump.

And it hit me then how lucky I was that I *could* run.

I reached the place at the edge of the woods. And there was the path to the pond, just where it had always been.

I put my hand to my mouth. Then I ran back to Gary. "The path was there, where it was before. So . . . why did we end up in the rose garden, then?"

"I told you. You panicked and you went the wrong way."

"There is no wrong way—there's no other path and

you know it!" I started pushing the chair again. "And it would be too hard to push this chair if we *weren't* on the path—especially as fast as I was going."

Gary shook his head. "I'm getting bored with this subject," he said.

I headed directly back toward the edge of the valley and the long avenue of flowering shrubs. Now I was pretty sure they'd be in the right places, too.

Could Gary possibly be right? Could I have run off the path, and not realized it? But with the chair, that wasn't physically possible. And I *had* been on a path. I was as sure of that as I was of anything in my life.

What had happened in the woods, anyway?

We passed the edge of the valley; we trundled along down the avenue of tall blossoming shrubs. Past the stone shed and the outhouse with its brilliant wild blossoms that never should have been there. And if Gary was right about the lotuses, these flowers wouldn't be here either when nobody was here to observe them. Did it even have to be a person? Would a bug looking at them make them appear?

And as we reached the orchard, Luke came strolling along. He was wearing his overalls and no shirt; you could see the wiry dark muscles on his shoulders and arms. His orange cat Sro-dee was perched on his shoulder, as usual. "Hello, Susan. Hello, Gary," he said, polite and smiling as he always was. "Hey, what's that you got there?" he asked Gary. "Never see any lotuses around here." He shook his head. "Wrong climate again. Another flower from my part of the world. Funny thing going on in this place, for sure." He was still smiling.

It was a relief that he agreed with me about that—if anybody knew about the garden, it was Luke. "The pond was full of them," I said.

"In Cambodia, we have story about lotus," Luke said. "Father bird go out in late afternoon to find food for babies. He sees lotus flower like that one and goes inside it to get insects there. He is very tired. And he forget that in the evening, the lotus flower close. You will see this happen if you keep it. So he fall asleep inside. The petals close around the bird and he can't get out all night. His wife think he don't come back because he is sleeping with a girlfriend, so she kill the babies and then kill herself. In the morning when the lotus open and the father bird can get out, he goes right home—and sees his wife and babies dead. So then he kill himself, too."

Great story, I thought. It just made the pond and the changing path seem even more sinister. "Maybe you should go and check out the pond—and the path coming back from it," I said to Luke.

"I go there when I got a minute," he said. "Got some serious weeding I got to do first. And, Susan, you better change your clothes—I bet you fall down in the pond." He smiled. "See you two later." And he walked past us toward the avenue of blossoms.

"Big help *he* was," I muttered as I pushed the chair out onto the lawn.

"He said funny things were going on around here," Gary said. "Isn't that what you wanted to hear?"

"You said it, too, only you don't remember," I reminded him.

He had no answer to that. He just said, "I'm going to keep this lotus and see if it closes up like Luke said."

Even though I had been expecting it to be in the right place, it was still a huge relief to see the house. I couldn't wait to get Gary back inside. I'd had enough of him for one day. And when Dad came home, I'd ask him about the path to the pond. Maybe he'd answer this time. Mom wouldn't know much; she hadn't grown up here, and as far as I could tell she didn't go into the woods very often herself. Anyway, her car wasn't there; she must have gone out shopping.

I pushed Gary up the ramp. It got easier every day. At the top I bumped open the screen door and wheeled Gary into the kitchen. There was a bag of potato chips on the table and two egg salad sandwiches in the fridge.

We could each eat our lunch whenever we felt like it. But first, the lotus.

The vases were on top of the kitchen cabinets and I had to get up on a chair to reach them. "Which one do you want?" I asked Gary.

He held up the lotus blossom, coughing a little, and then looked over the vases. "That Chinese-looking one with the dragons on it," Gary said. "Lotuses come from the Orient, like Luke said."

I got the vase down, rinsed it out, and filled it with water. It was just the right size for the blossom. Gary held it carefully as I wheeled him to the screened porch. He put it down on his bedside table. And then he picked up a book—a big book full of lavish pictures, all about flowers. It was the first time I had seen this book; I had never known he was interested in flowers. But clearly this book was why he had recognized the lotuses. He must have ordered it online.

I didn't ask Gary about the book; I didn't feel like any more of his weird, changeable answers. I needed something normal. I left him there with his book and his lotus and went up to my room. I took a quick shower and changed my clothes.

I wanted to talk to Lisa right away. I didn't want to wait to see if she was online, so I called her on the phone.

"Susan? What's up?" She seemed a little flustered. We IMed a lot, and talked at school, but I had never called her before.

I took a breath, wondering how she would react. "I was just thinking, maybe you could come over sometime, hang out here," I said to Lisa. "I don't think you've ever seen this place. It's pretty wild. Maybe you've heard about it."

"Well, I heard your place was pretty unusual, even a little weird. And . . . well, yeah, I'd like to see it. Thanks. It's just that . . ." She hesitated.

I knew what she was afraid to say. But she seemed more thoughtful than a lot of other people, and I might be able to persuade her. "You don't need to worry about my brother, Gary," I said. "I already took him out this morning. I'll be doing that every morning from now on. So if you come in the afternoon, we don't need to spend time with him. Anyway, he acts completely normal." That was a lie, but I hoped he wouldn't do anything that would put Lisa off.

"You're sure it's okay? I don't want to disturb him," she said.

Why was everybody so afraid of sick people? Wondering about that was what gave me the idea that might convince her. "I told you, his friends never come to see him," I said. "It's sad. And none of mine come either. And . . . I'm kind of stuck here."

"Why don't your other friends come to see you?" Lisa asked.

"They're all afraid, because Gary's sick." There; I'd actually said it. "And they're not the types to be interested in a garden, even a big one like ours. You're more like the kind of person who would appreciate it. I think you'd really be amazed."

There was a pause. "Er . . . sure. I'll come over," Lisa finally said.

She was hesitant, too. I had to arrange it right away, before she could think of an excuse. I looked at my watch. Gary and I had left early and it was still only lunchtime. After what had happened today, I felt like a break from the weirdness—and to be with somebody who wasn't Gary. "What about today? Right after lunch. I've already taken Gary for his walk, and the weather's great, and I'm . . . I'm really tired of being alone so much." I sort of hated playing on her pity, but I really, really wanted to be with a girl my own age, for a change.

"Well . . . sure." She still sounded a little hesitant, but at least she was agreeing.

"That's great!" I said.

"I can ride my bike over. How about if I get there in about an hour."

"See you then."

I went down and knocked on the screened porch door. "Yeah?" Gary said. "Come on in."

I stepped out onto the porch. I had to admit, the porch was beautiful in the daytime, with the front lawn on one side, and the big old trees surrounding the rest. It was like being outside, but protected. "You want me to bring your sandwich and chips out here? I'm eating now. And then a friend of mine's coming over."

"One of those slugs you hang out with? Aren't they afraid of seeing me in this thing?" he said, patting the chair. Then he put his hand to his mouth and coughed again.

"This is a different friend—Lisa. She's not the same as the others. Like, she reads."

"Gee, a real weirdo," Gary said sarcastically. Now I noticed that there were more books on the porch than there had ever been in his room upstairs. Someday when he wasn't in there I'd check them out. I wouldn't be surprised if they were mostly about gardens—and science.

"Yeah, bring the sandwich out here," Gary said. "I'm sort of tired after this morning. But I'd still like to meet this friend of yours."

"Well, we're going to go for a walk. She wants to see the garden." Now I wasn't so sure how Gary would act with Lisa; I didn't want him to scare her away. Still, he hadn't seen any other kids in weeks. And despite how inconsistent and weird—and nasty—he had been today, part of me still felt sorry for him. "But anyway, she'll come and say hello."

I went to get his sandwich.

What would Gary say to Lisa?

But before she met him I had to take her to the garden. I felt a sharp twinge of fear. I really didn't want to go back to the garden at all—I had used it as a bribe.

But now I knew why I had called Lisa. I needed somebody to share this with, somebody who wasn't Gary.

I got the sandwich out of the fridge and poured him a glass of milk. I put some potato chips into a bowl. I had to put the whole thing on a tray, so I could carry the pill dispenser, too.

And as I carried the tray toward the screened porch, I had a scary thought. What if I took Lisa to the pond? It would be a lot easier to get there without the wheelchair.

And then I could find out what would happen on the way back from the pond. And if it was anything weird again, Lisa would be my witness.

4

Mom came home with supermarket bags while I was eating my sandwich in the kitchen. "How's Gary?" she said immediately.

Should I tell her about the path moving? But she seemed so worried that I didn't want to make it worse, and she'd probably just have thought I was crazy anyway. I would wait until Dad came home—he was cooler.

"He's fine. He's having lunch on the porch. I picked him a strange flower from the pond. He really wanted it."

She didn't even thank me. "I'd better go sit with him," she said. "Would you put the groceries away?"

"Sure. Er . . . a friend of mine's coming over in a little while. I spent the whole morning taking Gary around the garden. And I'll bring her in to meet him."

She smiled, finally. "That's great, Susan. I'm glad." And she went out to the porch.

Mom was still out on the porch when the doorbell rang, which was just as well because then Lisa wouldn't immediately have to go through the obligatory questions parents always ask when they meet a new kid.

Lisa had short, flat, mousy brown hair and her bangs were wet from riding her bike over. "Come on in," I said.

She looked around at the log walls. "Jeez, I never knew anybody who lived in a log cabin," she said, as she stepped inside. She wore old cutoffs and a worn knit top.

"Some crazy ancestor of Dad's took off the siding and exposed the logs, and we just left it that way. And wait'll you see how big the garden is. All these developers want to buy it and make subdivisions," I said. I was about to add that Dad couldn't sell it until Gary got better, or died, but stopped myself in time—I didn't want to start off morbid.

"Lucky your family can afford it," she said. That was one of the reasons Lisa wasn't popular—she could be blunt.

"Well, it's not easy. But it's been in Dad's family for generations, it's this ancestral thing—and if they wait a little longer it will just be more valuable. Anyway, it's unique, so they want to hold onto it as long as possible."

Then we didn't know what to say. "You want a Coke or anything?" I said, to fill the silence.

"Maybe a glass of water. Then I'd like to see this garden." She followed me into the kitchen. "Looks like your parents aren't here. Is it okay to leave your brother at home alone?"

"My mom's with him. You can meet them later. He lives out on the screened porch now. He wants to be outside as much as possible."

"I read that about dying—er, I mean about sick people. For some reason they like to be outside."

"Yeah, well from now on I'll be taking him out in his wheelchair every day." I put some ice and some water from the fridge into a glass. "We were deep in the garden this morning." I wondered how I had the nerve to go back into the garden after what had happened. I couldn't have gone alone, for sure.

She gulped down the water and I put the glass in the dishwasher. "Well, might as well get going," I forced myself to say. I hoped the garden would break the ice and give us something to talk about. Lisa wasn't the type to talk about girl things like I did with my other friends, and I wasn't ready to start getting into boys with her. I knew Gary wanted to meet her, but that

could wait until later when she and I were more comfortable together, I hoped.

"This ramp must be for the wheelchair," she said as
we walked down it.

"Yeah, my dad made it. Since Gary got too weak to
walk."

She shook her head. "Seems lousy to me that his
friends don't come over now. Didn't he have close
friends?"

"He thought so. But he's too proud to talk about it."

"Have Valerie and Jen and those kids seen this garden?"

"They've been here, but they were never interested
in going far enough to see the deep parts. They preferred to listen to music and watch TV and talk. Normal
everyday things."

"Yeah" was all she said, but there was a lot of mean-
ing in it.

We had reached the orchard. "There's only about a
dozen apple trees here, but we've always called it the
orchard," I said.

"Are the apples any good?"

"I think they're sour and hard, but now Gary talks
about how they're the best apples." I shook my head.
"Wishful thinking, I guess."

That was another dead end to conversation—a person

who was probably dying would want to remember wishful, false things like that. And that was exactly what we both wanted to avoid talking about.

"The apple trees are beautiful in the spring, with all the blossoms," I said.

"I bet," she said, as we left the orchard and passed Luke's shed. This wasn't working out at all. Now that we weren't online or at school, it was apparent that we really didn't know each other very well and didn't have a lot in common. I had thought the garden would give us something to relate to, but it didn't seem to want to help me.

"Speaking of blossoms," Lisa said. "Look at those big red flowers around that wooden building on that little hill."

Should I tell her? Why not? It wouldn't matter what Lisa said to the other kids anyway, if she ever saw any of them, that is. "They weren't here until yesterday when I took Gary in here on his chair. Luke—he's the gardener—said they're not native to this climate. They grow in Cambodia, where he comes from."

She stopped and looked at me. "That's hard to believe. You're telling me they grew that big from nothing overnight?" she said.

"Uh huh." I nodded. "We were all surprised. Dad said that seeds blow around in the wind—even though there's never been flowers like that in the garden before, as long as I can remember." And I wondered suddenly, for the first time, if there was a connection between Gary's illness and what was happening in the garden.

"Your father grew up here, right?" Lisa asked me. "Did you bring him out here to see these flowers and ask him if *he'd* ever seen anything like them here before?"

That would have been a good idea and I wished I'd thought of it. But I hadn't told him until dinner, when it was getting dark. And he went to work early in the morning. "I should have," I said. "I'll bring him here when he comes home from work today. Good idea."

"How about your grandparents? They must remember all sorts of stuff about the garden. What have they told you?"

"I never really knew them. They went into nursing homes or overseas when I was little, and then I guess they died. At least that's what Mom and Dad said."

"There were no funerals or anything?" Lisa asked me. "No."

"That's really strange, don't you think?"

It had never struck me before that it *was* odd that we hadn't had funerals for them. I didn't even know where they were buried. In Europe? And after today, I couldn't help but wonder if it had something to do with the garden. Every new thought I had about the garden was sinister, and Lisa wasn't making it any better.

Luke was doing some much needed weeding in the long avenue of flowering shrubs. Sro-dee was sleeping nearby. "Luke, this is Lisa," I said. "Lisa, meet Luke. He takes care of the garden."

He smiled, as usual. "Better if you say I try to take care of garden," he said. "Too much for one man here. But it's the only thing I know how to do."

"I think you do great," Lisa said, as if she had seen more than a tiny bit yet.

"Thank you," he said. "Good to see more young faces around here again." He turned back to his work.

When we were out of earshot, Lisa said, "He's really cute. You said he's from Cambodia?"

"Yeah. Wherever that is."

"It's in Southeast Asia, in between Thailand and Vietnam. Eight hundred years ago it was the most powerful empire in the area, and the biggest. There are still huge Buddhist temples from that time. It was called the Khmer Empire. Now it's a lot smaller and really poor and in trouble. They had genocide. People are still always getting killed there. Luke is lucky to be here."

In a way she was showing off, telling me all this stuff she knew about the Khmer Empire, and I was reminded of why the other kids didn't like her. On the other hand, it really was interesting to know something about the country Luke came from, since I really liked Luke. I had no idea he was so lucky to be here. He didn't talk about the problems and dangers in Cambodia. The fact that he was always so pleasant despite a hard life made me see him differently.

We had reached the edge of the valley and the meadow. Now I had to decide. Did I dare to take the path to the pond, or did we just go look at the old greenhouse and the rose garden? I paused.

"Well, now where?" Lisa said, blunt as usual. But at least she was blunt in real life, and not just on the computer, like the others. Did that mean I could trust her?

Maybe I'd leave our destination up to fate, and see what she said. Then I wouldn't have to decide. "Well, we could go look at the old falling down greenhouse and the rose garden. Or we could go deep into the woods, near where the state park starts. It's dark, and there's a pond there where Dad's aunt drowned when she was a little girl." I wanted to make it sound as scary as I could.

"It's still early," Lisa said brightly, not sounding scared at all. "Can't we see everything?"

I stifled my sigh. "Well . . . yeah, there's time." I took a deep breath. It only made sense to do the pond first, while it was still the middle of the day and the light was brighter than it would be later.

"Okay. We better do the pond first." I turned right and we walked toward the dreaded path. I walked fast down the path in the woods, wanting to get it over with. She kept dawdling and looking around. "Yeah, it is kind of eerie in here. Hey, look at those cool mushrooms." She knelt down.

I had to kneel down, too, just to be polite. I wasn't interested in mushrooms—until I saw them. They were bright red and had little white dots on them. "Amanitas," Lisa said, sounding awed. "They're one of the most poisonous mushrooms in the world. You take a bite, you die."

Great, I thought. Just like the garden to have poisonous mushrooms in it. Gary would love to know about them and see them, of course. I hoped Lisa wouldn't tell him about them. I didn't want to take him back in here.

"*Lotuses?*" she said, as soon as we were close enough to see them. "But—they're tropical."

"Like those red flowers by the outhouse," I said. "They were never here before either. I don't know what it means, how it's possible. Gary says they're only here when someone is here to see them."

Lisa turned and looked at me, then back to the pond, frowning. "There's got to be some mistake," she said.

"For a second I thought they could be lotuses, but that's not possible. They've got to be some other plant that just looks like lotuses. Lotuses can't grow here."

I could have repeated what Luke had said about the red flowers, but I didn't feel like dawdling here. It was getting darker and darker now. Finally I managed to drag her away from the pond, back down the path. My heart was thudding again, I was so scared about where the path was going to end up.

Lisa kept seeing more of those poisonous mushrooms and exclaiming about them. I hardly listened, concentrating on the light at the end of the woods.

And when we reached it, the path was right where it belonged.

Had I imagined what had happened this morning? Or had it only happened because I was with Gary?

We started for the greenhouse. She was awed by it, and a little less awed by the rose garden, which wasn't nearly as fantastic. There was no path into the woods there anymore.

And suddenly I had to tell her, even though she hadn't believed about the lotuses and would probably think I was crazy. "This morning, when I took Gary to the pond, when we came back, the path from the pond ended up here, at the rose garden."

She looked at me, squinting. "Huh?"

"You can ask Gary, but he probably won't admit it. But I'm telling you, it's true. I'm not crazy. The path moved. And now it's moved back. It must be part of the other weird things—the lotuses and the red flowers growing overnight. Something's happening in the garden."

"What are you talking about?" she said.

"I know it sounds weird," I said, knowing *I* sounded weird. "But you saw the lotuses and they're impossible. And . . . do I seem like the kind of person who would, like, have hallucinations?"

"No, you don't. And you don't seem like the kind of person who would live in a log house or have a garden like this. But I still can't believe a path could move." She shook her head. "You imagined it, Susan. Maybe because you're worried about your brother." She lifted her hands, her mouth a hard line. A moment later she relaxed. "Still, I have to admit this is one of the most interesting afternoons I've ever had."

Now I didn't know what to think. I was almost disappointed the path hadn't moved again, because if Lisa had seen it, that would prove it had really happened. *Had* I imagined it, after all? But I had never imagined anything so realistic before in my life.

She looked at her watch. "We better go back if I'm going to have time to meet your mom—and your brother." She didn't sound too enthusiastic.

We started back. I was glad she was walking more quickly now. I had had way more than enough of the garden for one day.

"Still, it's strange that those flowers in the pond look so much like lotuses, and those red flowers look tropical, too," she admitted. "They never grew here before, as far as you know?"

"Never."

"Your brother got sick, and these things start to happen," she said slowly. "Do you think there might be some connection?"

I felt like hugging her, but of course I didn't. "Yes!" I practically shouted. "That's what I thought, too. I'm so glad you had the same idea. It makes me feel like I'm *not* crazy. Gary keeps talking about this as a quantum garden, and one of our relatives who built the garden was a quantum scientist. Maybe the combination of quantum and disease has something to do with what's happening to the garden."

She shrugged. "Well, it's peculiar. And quantum is very weird. But it's *tiny*. There's got to be some other, more realistic explanation for it. No matter what you think you saw, Susan."

"But Luke said they were lotuses, and he knows," I almost pleaded with her.

"Okay, it's peculiar. But there's got to be some explanation that isn't magic, like you seem to think." She sounded like she felt sorry for me for being delusional.

It was late afternoon now and Mom was in the kitchen cooking. They said all the usual things. Then I asked Mom, "Would it be okay if Lisa met Gary? I mean if he's not too tired."

Mom fell all over herself with eagerness. She practically pushed us out to the screened porch. And she didn't even come out onto the porch with us—she was smart enough to know that Gary would have a better time if there were no adults there for this rare occasion of another kid visiting him.

He looked up from his book. I could see right away that this book wasn't about flowers—there were equations in it, not photographs. He closed it and shoved it aside as soon as we came in. I introduced them. "Sit down, sit down," Gary said, gesturing at the chair and the bed.

Since I was his sister, I sat on the bed.

"You went to the garden, right?" he asked us.

"It's incredible," Lisa said, leaning forward in her chair.

Gary looked very pleased.

Lisa saw the lotus in the vase right away. "That must be from the pond," she said. "You went into the water and picked it?" she asked me.

All I did was nod. I didn't want to tell her Gary had made me do it, right in front of him.

"It looks different from the other ones, like it's closing up," Lisa said. "Is it withering out of the water or something?"

I waited, to see if Gary would tell her Luke's story. And he did. He had never been interested in my friends before, but Lisa was the first person close to his age he had seen in a while, and he was eager.

Lisa wrinkled her nose. "*That's* the kind of stories they tell in Cambodia? About death. And about such a beautiful flower."

Lisa was blunt all right. There was a stunned silence as it sank in that she had said the word that nobody ever mentioned. And so to fill the silence I told her something that Gary might consider a betrayal. "Gary said the lotus would make him stronger."

I didn't know what Gary felt about me telling her that, because he didn't say anything. But with Lisa around that didn't matter. "Well, it *does* make a certain sense," she said. "It's impossible that they would grow there in the first place. So there's a warped logic that they'd have a kind of magical strength about them. That is, if you believe they really are lotuses, which they can't be."

"Luke said they were, and he would know," Gary told her, just as I had. "And how did you know it's impossible for lotuses to grow in this climate, anyway?"

"Remember what I told you about Lisa?" I said. "She *reads*. You should hear what she told me about Cambodia."

"Yeah?" he said, and she told him.

He looked at me. "Luke never told us any of that stuff," he said. He paused. "When you think about it, Luke never says much about himself at all. Just the garden. We don't know a thing about his family. That story about the bird getting trapped in the lotus and his wife killing herself and their kids is the closest he's come to saying anything at all about where he comes from. And it's just a folktale."

"Funny," Lisa said. "Do you think he's hiding anything? Like maybe he's an illegal immigrant or something and he's afraid the government will catch him and deport him back to Cambodia? They're tough and they're getting tougher. And they make it especially hard for people from places like Cambodia, places everybody wants to get away from."

"Well, maybe I'll ask Dad," Gary said. He turned to look at the lotus. "But Luke was right about this flower, anyway. Look. You can practically see it closing up."

He was right. The tops of the petals were almost

touching now.

Lisa looked at her watch. She still didn't want to believe it was really a lotus. "Oh! It's later than I thought. I have to go. But . . . I'd like to come back, if that's okay." She looked back and forth between us.

"Sure, anytime," Gary said immediately, without giving me a chance to say anything. I didn't like that.

"Can you tell me where the bathroom is?" she said, as we stepped inside from the porch into the old living room. "Wow, look at that fireplace. It's plenty big enough to walk into."

"There's a newer bathroom downstairs, but the upstairs one is more interesting," I said, leading her up the wooden stairway.

She rested her hand on the railing. "Hey, this thing is all tongue-and-groove. No nails at all. This place is amazing."

I didn't mention that I had never noticed there were no nails in the staircase railing.

The upstairs bathroom was another oddity of the house, created by yet another eccentric relative—or maybe the same Uncle Arthur who had won the Lebon Prize for quantum physics. The unusual part was the shower. It was almost like a piece of sculpture, made out of carved, glazed ceramic tiles. It was round, and when you were in it it was as though you were in a kind of tropical marsh. Ceramic grasses and flowers grew up from the floor along the walls, and some of them were actually lotuses, I noticed for the first time. There were also animals worked into the tiling, big frogs with yellow glassy eyes, and brightly plumped flamingos balancing on one spindly leg, and a sky with rain clouds looming, and flying birds, and a partially hidden sun. None of my other friends had paid much attention to it, when they came to visit me up in my room, but Lisa was absolutely fascinated. "This has got to be the most amazing house I've ever seen," she kept saying.

She didn't take very long, unlike most girls—she probably didn't even look in the mirror. She came bursting out of the bathroom when I was still only halfway down the stairs, wondering if there was a connection between the lotus in the bathroom and the ones in the garden.

"Hey, why didn't you take me to that maze?" she said from the top of the stairs. "I thought you were going to show me the whole garden."

I started hoping again. The maze was the weirdest thing in the garden by far—it might help Lisa believe me aobut the other stuff.

"Come and look," she urged me.

I hurried back up the stairs. She beckoned me into the bathroom, and over to the window, and pointed.

"Oh, yeah, those hedges," I said. I had stopped wondering long ago why we could never find the intricate maze of hedges that seemed to be in a clearing in the woods. "We've never been there. I don't know where they are, exactly. You can only see them from this one window."

She was staring at me with her mouth half-opened. "Wait a minute," she said. "You've lived here for your whole life, and you could always see that hedge maze from this window, but you've never actually *been* to it?"

"As far as I know, nobody has. You can see it from this window but you can't get there. It used to bother Gary, and he used to try, but my father sort of didn't encourage him, and eventually he just gave up."

She shook her head at me in disbelief. "But . . . but aren't you curious about this totally weird optical illusion? Something in your own garden that you can see from only one window and can't get to? It's one of the weirdest—and scariest—things I've ever seen in my life. You've never gotten your father to take you there? To explain what it's for, and who planted it, or anything?"

"He never wants to talk about it. I mean, after a while you give up, if something seems impossible."

"You never told anybody else about it—anybody not in the family? None of your friends ever noticed when they were here?"

I shook my head.

"They must have been too busy looking in the mirror," she said, and stomped almost angrily out of the room. She went down the stairs ahead of me, not looking back at me as she talked. "Maybe . . . maybe you're not imagining things after all," she admitted, and I felt a surge of relief. "If there's no way to get to that maze, and you can only see it from that one window, that *proves* something weird's going on in the garden. You think I could come back tomorrow and we could try to find the maze?" she said. "Maybe we could bring Gary, too. Would your mother mind?"

I knew my mother wouldn't mind, because obviously Gary would relish spending time with someone new, even Lisa. The question was, would *I* mind? I was glad she was starting to believe I wasn't imagining things. But did I really want Lisa barging in and prying into this thing that we had all just come to accept—and that my father obviously didn't want us to think about?

"Well," I said, hesitating, coming down slowly as she waited impatiently at the bottom of the stairs. "Well, my mother knows Gary likes having visitors." And I was thinking that having somebody else along, even Lisa, would probably be better than being alone with Gary all the time. "But I don't know about my father,"

I said, lowering my voice. "It's like—we always knew he never wanted us to even try to find the maze. And like, his aunt Caroline drowning in the pond . . . something worse might have happened in the maze and that's why it's so hard to find, and why he never wanted us to try to get there."

"Does he have to know?" Lisa whispered.

5

For a while it had been a relief to be with Lisa, when she had finally agreed with me that the garden was acting weird, and that it might have something to do with Gary's illness. It had also been good to have somebody else to be with Gary, instead of him depending on me as his only companion.

But I was glad when she left. I didn't like the way she was so curious about the maze. Dad had never actually told Gary *not* to try to find it—that would have encouraged him to look for it harder than ever. Dad had just been totally vague and noncommittal about it, the same way he was when I asked him if anything else bad had happened in the garden besides his aunt Caroline drowning. Over the years we had stopped thinking about the maze. And I didn't want to start thinking about it now. If an ordinary path could end up in the wrong place, then what on earth would happen in a *maze*, a place designed to confuse you? I didn't want to have anything to do with it.

Lisa also made me feel like I didn't know much about anything.

And just before she left, outside the door where no one else could hear, I told her it probably wouldn't be a good idea for her to come over the next day. Gary had already had a huge amount of excitement for one day, and he probably needed a day of calmness and rest. She squinted at me but didn't argue, and got on her bike and rode away.

It was too bad I had to tell her that. But I didn't want to go fooling around with the maze. Lisa had to understand that if she wanted to spend more time here.

The one good thing was that Lisa hadn't said anything to Gary about the maze—she hadn't seen it until she was about to leave. If she had mentioned it to him, he might have gotten all interested in it again and forced me to wheel him around for hours looking for it. He was so different these days that I never knew what crazy fixations he would get into his head.

I made sure to be downstairs when Dad came home. He went straight out to the screened porch, and I went with him. He saw the lotus right away. "Where did

Mom find that?" Dad wanted to know. "I didn't know any florists around here sold flowers like that."

"Mom didn't buy it," Gary said. "The pond is full of them. It happened all of a sudden. And . . . Susan went into the water and picked it for me."

Gary had kept his promise about telling them what I had done; I had to give him credit for that.

Now Dad was doubly surprised. He *had* to think it was strange about the red flowers and now the lotuses. But—as usual with the garden—he didn't want to make a big deal out of it. So instead he focused on me. "But, Susan, you hate the pond. You didn't actually go into the water and pick it, did you?"

Now I couldn't resist. Even though Gary had told Dad I had picked the lotus, I was still mad at him for telling Lisa to come back anytime without waiting for me to say anything. And I was mad at Dad for being so secretive about the garden, and whether or not it really was dangerous. "Yes, I did go into the water," I said. "Gary asked me to pick a lotus for him. He said it would make him stronger to have it here on his porch with him."

"You keep saying I said that," Gary said. He really was tired, and sounded whiny. "But I don't remember it."

"You were . . . different when we were at the pond."

"It might be a good idea not to go there anymore,"

Dad said, trying to squirm away from our disagreement.

"But did lotuses ever grow there before?" I asked him, enjoying putting him on the spot. "I think something weird is going on."

He sighed, as though he didn't want to answer. "Well, not lotuses . . ." He paused. And then he said, "It's not a big deal. Like those red flowers around the outhouse you were telling me about. Seeds blow in the wind."

But Gary wasn't taking it. Being tired made him more ornery. "Yeah, but I've been reading about flowers," he said. "Lotuses only grow in the tropics. This is Massachusetts. It's too far north. Susan's right. Something weird *is* going on."

I was surprised that Gary was sticking up for me for a change. "If it's too late to go to the pond, maybe you could come with me and look at those flowers around the outhouse," I said to Dad.

"Well . . . ," he said doubtfully, checking his watch.

"Yeah, why don't you go?" Gary said. "I'm too tired, but you really should see them."

Dad sighed. A request from me he could ignore, but not one from his sick son.

"It'll only take you a minute or two, without bringing me along," Gary urged him.

"Okay, okay," Dad said, standing up. "But only for a minute. It's almost dinnertime."

Dad and I walked out together. "That's true what you said, about Gary saying the lotus would make him stronger?" he asked me as we walked across the lawn toward the darkening orchard.

"Yeah. He was strange when we were at the pond, like in a kind of trance—the things he said, his voice, everything." It felt good to tell somebody who knew Gary, even though I was mad at Dad.

We walked under the long shadows of the apple trees, the leaves rustling. "What else did he say?" Dad asked me, reluctantly, as though he felt he had to but he really didn't want to know.

"I'll tell you at dinner," I said. I wanted Mom to be there, too, and Gary, so I could get all their reactions. We left the apple trees behind and approached the stone shed and the outhouse. "See?" I said. "You ever see flowers like that before?" And then I felt a pang. "They're taller than when I was here with Lisa this afternoon."

Dad stopped and looked at them. I could almost see the effort he was making to keep his expression perfectly blank. "No, I never did see any flowers like that here before," he said, and shrugged, as though it didn't make any difference. "But that doesn't mean a whole lot. I didn't inherit the gardening gene. For all I know they might come up every five years and I just never noticed."

"But Luke said they don't grow in this part of the world, just in the tropics—like what Gary said about the lotuses."

"And that's not all," a soft voice said from behind us, in the fading light. Dad and I both jumped, and turned. It was Luke. He had come along so quietly it almost seemed like he was sneaking up on us. Sro-dee watched us from his shoulder.

"They are not just any tropical flowers," Luke continued. It was hard to tell in the shadows if he was smiling or not. "They are poppies—opium poppies. People make drugs out of them—illegal drugs. People who start using those drugs can't stop. I have seen it many times. It might be best if I dug them up by the roots and burned them, and made it so they will never—"

Dad lifted his hand. "No," he said with finality. "Leave them. Maybe there's a reason they came up. Just destroy the real weeds."

Luke bowed his head. "As you wish. Or maybe . . . you would like me to harvest them and take the drug from them? It makes pain go away. And maybe if Gary is in pain . . ."

I could hardly believe Luke had actually said that. "Just don't do anything," Dad said. "Come on, Susan. It's time for dinner." He turned abruptly and started back toward the house. "Who's Lisa?" he asked me, when we were far enough away from the shed so Luke wouldn't hear. "You said she was with you this afternoon. You've never mentioned her before. I'm glad your friends are coming over here again. But . . ."

He didn't finish the sentence. "But what?" I asked him. It almost sounded as though he didn't want me to bring people to the garden any more.

"Oh, nothing," he almost snapped at me. "Gary's friends used to like to play in the garden, but yours never did. It just seems strange that all of a sudden . . ." His voice faded again.

We walked back to the house in silence.

We moved Gary from his wheelchair to his chair at the table, the pill dispenser next to his plate. Everybody was there. And so after we started eating I said, "Dad, how many paths are there through the woods to the pond?"

"That's a funny question," he said, not knowing what this was leading to. "We all know there's only one."

"Then there's no path that starts at the pond and goes straight to the rose garden, right?"

He gave me a strange look. "Of course not. What a funny thing to ask."

I turned to Gary. "Tell them what happened today. When we came back from the pond after I picked the lotus for you."

Gary was really tired now, and even more ornery. "Sure, I'll tell them," he said. "When Susan was in the pond picking the lotus a bird screamed, and she got scared and fell in. She freaked out and pushed the chair out of the woods much too fast, and went the wrong way and we came out of the woods at the rose garden. She kept saying there was something crazy about it, that the path didn't go that way. But she was just freaking out."

I was furious. I had done him this huge favor and then this impossible thing had happened and now he was making it sound like I was just being hysterical. I slammed my fork down on the table. "Yeah, I was scared. Everybody knows I hate the pond and I went into it to get you your precious lotus. But I did *not* leave the path." I looked back and forth between Mom and Dad. "You've both pushed that wheelchair. You know it would be impossible to push it through the woods if you weren't on the path. I never left the path. And it came out of the woods at the rose garden." I was breathing hard. "The path *moved*."

Mom and Dad had to force themselves to look away from each other and back to me. "Susan, dear," Mom said, as though she were talking to a four-year-old, "I know this is a difficult situation for all of us. But the only way we're going to get through it is to be strong, and keep a grip on reality."

I couldn't stand it. "And when we were at the pond, Gary said the garden was changing. He said weird things were happening and that's how Dad's family had planned it from the beginning and now it was finally coming true. And now he says he never said that. Gary!" I raised my voice. *"Where did the path come out of the woods?"*

"At the usual place," he said matter-of-factly, contradicting what he had said a minute ago.

"You're lying! A minute ago you said we came out at the rose garden."

"How can a path move?" Gary said.

I jumped up from the table. "You're a liar!" I shouted. "I'm never taking you there again!"

"Don't talk to your brother like that, Susan!" Mom ordered me.

I ran upstairs and slammed the door of my room and threw myself down on the bed. I didn't want them to see me crying.

I knew it was hard to believe. I also knew it had really happened. Did they think I was crazy? They were always on Gary's side now because he was sick.

Or else . . . . maybe I *was* crazy.

There was the inevitable knock on the door. "Susan?"

Dad said.

"Go away."

"Suze. What if I said . . . you might not be entirely wrong."

Should I let him lie and try to placate me? Or should I just sulk? But I was curious to hear what he would come up with. And sulking was boring. I wiped my eyes on the pillowcase. "Okay. You can come in."

He sat down on the edge of the bed but he didn't try to take my hand or anything. "I know this is hard for you, with Gary getting all the attention, and you having so much responsibility. I also know the garden is an odd place. I'm not a scientist like Great-Uncle Arthur, but I do know there are things in the world that sometimes don't seem to make sense. Try to be patient with Gary. He might understand more than he lets on. He's dealing with a lot of hard issues right now. The more you're his friend, the more he might understand the way you see things."

"I know what happened and he does, too, and he won't admit it."

"The only way you'll come to an agreement is by being patient. Neither one of you is unreasonable. Come on down and make up. That'll be better for everybody."

I sighed. "But . . . but he . . ."

"Just let it rest for the time being. See what happens tomorrow. Getting angry isn't going to help anything."

"I won't take back what I said."

"You don't have to. Just let it be for the time being. Okay? I promise you'll feel better. And everything will be cleared up soon. You've been doing great."

So I went downstairs and ate with them. We talked about Luke and Cambodia. Dad was impressed with how much Lisa knew, and thought she sounded like an intelligent person and decided he was glad she had come over after all. He also insisted that Luke was not an illegal alien—he had all the necessary papers. "It wouldn't be worth the risk to employ him if he didn't," Dad said. He was probably right. I was pretty sure he was bending the tax laws in order to be able to afford not to sell off the garden, and he wouldn't want to do anything else that might draw attention to that.

"Do you think those flowers are really opium poppies?" I asked him.

"Huh?" Gary said, perking up. "Luke said that? I wonder why I didn't recognize them. After supper I'm going to look it up."

"Sure. But don't tell this Lisa person or anybody else," Dad cautioned us.

When we'd finished eating, we put Gary back in his chair and I wheeled him out to the porch. Mom and

Dad left us alone. And in fact Gary did find a picture of opium poppies and they looked exactly like the flowers around the outhouse.

"I'm not surprised. Of course that's something Luke would know," Gary said. His eyes moved over to the lotus. The petals were tightly pressed together now, forming a closed, rounded shape. "He was right about that too." Gary yawned. "I'm going to fall asleep in this chair in a minute. It's been a long day."

I got Dad and we put him to bed. Dad left us alone again before Gary turned out the light. "What's quantum?" I asked Gary.

"Are you going to tell me I was talking about that, too?"

I didn't want to get into another argument. "I'm just curious," I said.

"It's about the way things are on the tiniest levels— like the atomic level and smaller. These things control the physical world. It's really different there—unpredictable, counterintuitive."

"Sort of like . . . the garden?" I dared to say, hoping he wouldn't decide to argue with me again.

"That's what I'm starting to think," he said, and yawned again. I thought of bringing up the path when he was in this more accepting mood, but didn't. I left as he moved to turn off the light.

• • •

I was awakened just as it was getting light, by a screeching from the screened porch and a wild battering sound.

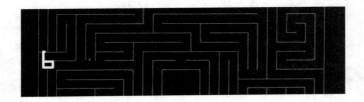

Mom and Dad and I were all on the stairs at the same time, fumbling into bathrobes. We rushed for the porch.

Gary was sitting up in bed, cringing back against the headboard. A million little brown birds with white wing tips were careening around the room, battering themselves against the screens in a desperate attempt to get out. And yet, at the same time, they seemed to be only half there; they were like a cloud.

I looked immediately at the lotus. The petals had opened in the dawn light.

"Did they come out of the lotus?" I screamed, my hands up against my face in case one of the crazed birds got near me.

"It must have," Gary said. "The door's been locked all

night."

"Open the door and get them out of here, Dave!" Mom shouted.

"No! Don't move!" Gary shouted, his throat taught. "It's too dangerous. Just stay where you are. If it hits you it could really hurt you."

"Why do you keep saying 'it'?" I screamed at him. "The whole porch is full of them!"

"It's really only one," Gary said. "It's everywhere and nowhere at the same time."

"What are you—?" Dad started to say.

And then suddenly the birds were gone. They weren't inside the porch any more. A brown cloud zigzagged over the trees in the valley.

"What on earth?" Mom said, sagging against the living room doorway.

"How in the world did they get in here?" Dad wanted to know. "What were you saying about the lotus?"

"It was a story Luke told, when he first saw the lotus," Gary said, and briefly repeated it.

"Are you trying to tell me all those birds got into that flower and were stuck there all night?" Dad said, sounding almost angry.

Gary shrugged. "I never saw it go in. But where else could it have come from?"

"Now do you believe me about the path?" I couldn't

stop myself from saying. "That isn't any crazier than this."

"I think we should all go back to bed and try to get some more sleep," Dad said. "We'll never know how they got in here or how they got out, and there's no point in trying to guess. We just have to make sure the doors are always locked from now on."

"It leaked out of the porch," Gary said. "Electrons can do that."

"It's too early for this craziness," Dad said. "We're all going back to bed. That's an order."

Of course I didn't get any more sleep, and I didn't think anybody else did either. We had breakfast earlier than usual. Gary was hungrier than usual, too—he had two soft-boiled eggs instead of one, and two pieces of toast. Mom was so pleased she stopped worrying about the bird, or the birds, or whatever it was. She didn't even notice that I was too nervous to eat anything. And I wasn't going to let Gary off without an explanation. He seemed to understand a lot more about everything than he was saying.

Still, for once Gary and I were in agreement about one thing, without even having to say it. We were both sure the crazy bird had come out of the lotus. We also knew there was no point in trying to convince Mom and Dad of that fact. They both obviously wanted to pretend the whole incident hadn't happened.

After Dad left for work and I took Gary out, he wanted to find Luke and tell him first thing. I did, too.

On the way there, still feeling panicky, my hands shaking a little on the chair handles, I said, "Gary, you said it was only one bird, even though they seemed to be everywhere. And you said it *leaked* out of the porch. What does that mean?"

"That's how electrons are, inside atoms," he said. "They're a wave, like on the ocean, and a particle, like a grain of sand in the wind, both at the same time. I told you quantum was weird."

"But what did you mean about how it *leaked* out of the porch?" I pressed him.

"Tiny objects can leak out of things without going through a window or a door, or any kind of opening. It's because atoms, which everything in the world is made of, are mostly empty space. You must have learned in school that an atom is a nucleus surrounded by a cloud of electrons. Let's say the nucleus was the size of a pinhead, floating in the middle of a huge cathedral. If it was that size, the cloud of electrons would be spinning around *outside* the cathedral. In a real atom, the cathedral isn't there, and everything in between the nucleus and the electrons is empty space. Most of the world is empty space at the atomic level, and hardly anything is solid. Also, the solid things have wildly fluctuating amounts of energy. Suddenly a particle can just develop enough energy, for a short period of time, to zip through the empty space from one object into another. That's why things down there can leak out of other things. Only it never, never happens with anything as big as that bird. Only with things that are too small to see." His cheeks were glowing. "It's like, normally you'd have to wait the life of the universe for something like what that bird did to happen at this big a level. But now it's happening *here*."

"But if it could leak out of the porch, why didn't it leak out of the lotus?"

He shrugged. "That I don't know. Maybe because there's something weird about the lotus because it's not supposed to be here in the first place."

We reached the shed. "I'll tell you more later," Gary said.

The poppies around the outhouse were so abundant now that they would have blocked the door if Luke had not cut some of them down.

"See if he's here," Gary said, as though nothing was wrong.

"But look at the poppies."

"Maybe they're quantum poppies, like the bird. Just see if Luke is here."

I knocked on the shed door. We waited. There was no response.

"He probably gets up really early. I think gardeners do that," Gary said. "Should we . . . see if the door's unlocked?"

Luke had lived here as long as we could remember, and we had never been inside the shed where he slept. This felt like an invasion of his privacy. But I was curious.

I knocked again and waited. Then I tentatively pushed at the door. It began to open. The big deadbolt on it had not been locked. I stopped. "This feels funny," I said.

"If he doesn't lock it, that must mean he doesn't care if people go in," Gary said. "I mean, somebody else might want a tool sometime."

"But . . ."

"Just hurry up and see if there's anything unusual inside," Gary told me.

I pushed open the door and went in. The shed had not been designed as a living space, and the windows were small. I could barely see a thing at first. But slowly my eyes adjusted. I was impatient in case Luke might come back, but there was no obvious light switch.

The rakes and shovels and pruning shears and buckets and hoses and bags of fertilizer were neatly hung up or stored in wooden shelves along the walls. Near one wall was a narrow bed, more like a cot. Between the bed and the wall was a low shelf with some candles on it and sticks of incense in jars and a little statue I could not identify. I looked around again quickly, but I was nervous and got out of there.

I was glad to see that Luke had not returned. "Well?" Gary said.

"Nothing unusual except some kind of little shrine with candles and incense."

"How are we going to find Luke?" Gary wondered. "Where would he be now? Do you know if he has any kind of schedule, or pattern?"

"Not that I know of," I said.

It was an exhausting morning. Luke didn't seem to be anywhere. Finally there was no place else to look but the pond—Gary's suggestion, of course.

"But why would he be at the pond?" I argued. "There's no gardening to do there."

"Don't worry, I'm not going to ask you to pick another lotus or anything," Gary said. "The one I have is still fresh and doing what it's supposed to do."

"Yeah, but . . . it seems like a long way to go for nothing."

"There's nothing to be afraid of, Suze," he said sarcastically. He had stopped being excited about the bird and was back to his normal self.

Now I really didn't want to take him there. "Why don't we just wait for Luke back at the shed? He's got to go back there sometime."

But Gary was the invalid. And that gave him power. So there I was again, pushing the chair through the horrible dark woods, worrying about what was going to happen to the path on the way back. "I'm not coming here again tomorrow," I said, as we crossed over the little bridge. "You can't make me. And Dad doesn't think it's such a great idea to come here. You heard him say it."

"Dad doesn't know everything. Just don't freak out again and it will be okay."

I stopped, and shook the wheelchair, hard. "I'm not going a step further until you admit that we ended up at the rose garden when we came back from here yesterday."

For a second Gary almost looked scared. It gave me a kind of thrill. He sighed. "Okay, okay, whatever you say."

"Will you tell Mom and Dad I was right?"

"Just keep going. It'll be over with faster. And then we'll see what happens."

Luke was just turning away as we approached the pond, but when he saw us he turned back. Gary made a low whistle. "Will you look at that," he whispered. His voice was already getting husky, the way it had been when we were here before.

You could hardly see any water at all now; it was completely covered by the big, flat, round leaves that surrounded the lotus blossoms. In fact, it was hard to tell where one leaf ended and another began; they made a solid cover over the surface of the water.

"It was not like this yesterday?" Luke softly asked.

"There's about twice as many here today," Gary told him.

For a moment the three of us just looked at the pond in silence. "Is that how fast they normally grow? And the poppies, too?" Gary finally asked him.

"Not normal they are here." Luke shook his head.

I wanted to get away from here. And I wanted Luke to come with us, in case the path went to a different place again. "Can we please go back—"

"Do people ever eat lotuses?" Gary interrupted me, in his strange monotone.

"Yes, people where I come from eat lotus. Some people think it is a kind of medicine, good for the stomach." He turned back to the pond and gestured at it with one brown hand. "But this, growing here so fast like this. I think dangerous to eat it."

"But what if I tried it?" Gary said. "What if it was

like a medicine that would help me get better?"

"I do not think so," Luke said unwaveringly. "Can not stand here all day. Too much work to do in this garden." He turned to go back down the path.

"Wait. We're going with you," I said, trying not to panic, beginning to turn the chair around in the soft earth next to the pond.

"Can't you just get me one more lotus, Suze?" Gary pleaded with me. "It would be easier today, there's so many more of them. They must be quantum lotus, growing so fast. The real quantum world is infinitely faster than the world we know. Up here at these sizes everything takes forever in comparison normally."

What was he talking about? "We're going back with Luke. He said it would be dangerous to eat those lotuses and he knows more than you do." I pushed the chair all the way around and hurried after Luke. "Luke. Wait! We're coming with you."

Being an invalid gave Gary a certain control. But it gave me the final control.

Luke stopped and waited for us to catch up with him, to my great relief. "The same about those poppies," Luke said. "Normal poppies already bad enough. Ones growing so fast probably even worse."

"How do you know?" Gary asked him. "Why does quantum have to be bad?"

"I don't know what is this quantum. Only thing I know about is plants. I know what is supposed to happen and what is not. And none of this is supposed to happen. Stay away. Things like this can hurt you. *Especially* you, Gary."

"Why especially me?" Gary said darkly, out of his tranquil pond mood already. He always hated admitting he was sick, even though he was in a wheelchair. And then he remembered something, and brightened. "Luke. We were going to tell you. You'll never guess what came out of the lotus on my porch this morning."

"Let me help with wheelchair, please, Susan," Luke said, though he was too polite to nudge me away from the handles. I thought maybe he was changing the subject because he didn't want to hear what Gary was going to say next.

And somehow, as much work as it was, I wanted to be in control of the chair. I knew it was making me stronger, and Luke was already plenty strong enough. "It's better if I push it," I said.

"Are you sure, Susan?" Luke said kindly.

"The garden is your job. This is mine," I said. It was nice of him to offer. But now that it came right down to it, I wanted my job.

I had to give it an extra push now. We were crossing the wooden bridge. Halfway there. I was actually *hop-*

ing the path would end up in the wrong place, so that Luke would experience it, too. Then, with Luke on my side, I would have proof.

"Luke!" Gary said more insistently. "You wouldn't believe what came out of the lotus on my porch this morning."

Now Luke had to deal with it. "I hope you are not going to tell me—"

"A bird!" Gary said, with triumph. "As soon as the lotus opened, there was a bird flying around crazily in the porch, banging against the screens, trying to get out. Everywhere and nowhere at the same time. A quantum bird. Right, Susan?"

"Yes," I said. "Mom and Dad and I heard it and woke up and ran down and there was this bird flying around on Gary's porch. Only it was like a million birds. And then suddenly it just leaked out."

Luke stopped walking and stared at both of us. His expression seemed stern. I had never seen him look that way before. "But bird falling asleep in lotus is only story," he said, his hands held tightly behind his back. "How can it really happen?"

"You said there are insects inside the lotus flower," Gary argued. "It makes sense that birds would go inside to eat them. Isn't that where the story came from?"

Luke turned away and started walking again. "How you feel the last two or three days, Gary?" he asked him. "You feel better or worse?"

Gary lifted his chin defiantly. "Better!" he said. "Today I had two eggs and two pieces of toast. Usually I only want one of each. Isn't that right, Susan?"

"Yeah, he ate more for breakfast. Mom loved it." But it was still obvious that Gary was thinner than ever.

Luke smiled. But it was a different kind of smile than his usual one. His usual one was a brightening and lifting of his whole face. This one was a curling of the lips. "Very happy, Gary," he said. "But I hope you do not believe my story about bird too much."

"All I know is that there was a quantum bird flying around in my room this morning when the lotus opened," Gary said.

"Do not think about story. Think about eating *two* sandwich for lunch," Luke said, smiling that nervous unreal smile again. He thought the garden was dangerous for Gary, and I knew that Gary thought it was good for him.

Luke understood about plants, in his own way. How much did Gary know? He had been reading so much recently, and looking up so many things on the internet.

More sunlight brightened the pine needles on the

ground now. That meant we were approaching the end of the woods.

The light hit us full in the face. We stepped out of the trees.

And then I was being pulled by the wheelchair down a steep slope, among pink and blue phlox and other wildflowers. Light as Gary was, the wheelchair was too heavy for me on this slope. If it hadn't been for Luke, I would have lost control.

The path from the pond had taken us directly to the top of the valley. Another place where it had never gone before.

Luke's hands gripped the rubber handles next to mine as we struggled to keep the chair from plunging down the steep slope, and crashing into a tree or tipping over on a rock. Gary was slipping forward in the chair, and I let go of the handles and held onto his bony shoulders to keep him in place. Luke was strong enough to bring the chair to a stop before it went very far down. Now that the chair was under control, I let go of Gary and pushed back on the ends of the hand rests as Luke pulled the chair back. Gary swayed uncomfortably and gripped the hand rests above where I was pushing them. After a few moments of effort and heavy breathing, we were back up to the meadow.

It was studded with wildflowers like never before.

"Quantum wildflowers, too," Gary said pleasantly, as though we hadn't just saved him from plunging down the hill into a tree.

I was more curious than ever about this quantum business, especially if it could explain what was happening to the garden. But now didn't seem exactly the right time. My heart was still pounding. "Aren't you even a little bit scared?" I couldn't keep from asking Gary. "You could have been hurt really bad. And it was the same path that dumped us in the rose garden."

"A quantum path," Gary murmured, looking pleased, and not scared at all.

I turned to Luke, giving Gary a quick, sharp little push. "This path is the only path in the woods. It always used to lead to another place in the meadow, over there, where it starts. It went from there to the pond and back again. You know that. But last time Gary and I came back on it, it went to the rose garden. This time it went to the valley." My voice was hoarse; I was pleading with him. "You were here, Luke. You were part of it happening, right? You'll stand up for me that this happened?"

"I have to go back to my room and think alone" was all Luke would say. "And you two go back to your house now, and stay there. Come on. I'll walk with you to the orchard. You should be safe from there."

We walked back with him. And before he went to his shed, he said to Gary, "Do not do anything crazy. Do not eat anything you are not supposed to eat. You hear me? I know more about these things than you do."

"Okay, okay," Gary said, though it was clear to me he didn't mean it. Even sick, he was as stubborn as he had ever been.

Luke turned and walked back to his shed. He went inside and we heard the click of the deadbolt.

I remembered the little shelf with the candles and the incense and the statue, and figured maybe he would be praying, to whatever he believed in. And it hit me then that I really was amazingly ignorant about Luke, after what Lisa had told me about Cambodia. I felt both angry about it, and chastened. Knowing more about Luke and where he had come from was an opportunity that somebody like Lisa would probably have gotten a lot of interesting stuff from, and that I knew nothing about.

I pushed Gary across the lawn. "You saw it yourself, *again*. This time the path dumped us into the valley. Are you going to keep on denying it?"

"What's the point of telling anybody else about it?" he said. "Mom and Dad will never believe it; they'll think we're crazy. The same way they didn't want to think about the bird. And if it ever happened to them, they'd think it was a hallucination."

He might be right about that. "But what did you mean about a quantum path? Why do you think everything weird is quantum?"

"I can try to explain. It's famously hard to understand. They say if you're not infuriated by quantum theory then you don't really understand it."

"Well I want to try. That's all I'm——"

Mom came running out of the house. "Thank God you finally came back! Gary, it's time for your transfusion. In all the excitement this morning I forgot. We have to go right now."

Of course I had to go, too, to help with Gary and the wheelchair. No more about quantum until later.

At least at the transfusion clinic there was a chance I'd learn a little more about what was wrong with Gary, and what his odds were.

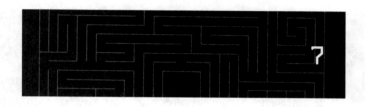

We didn't have to eat lunch, because
they had sandwiches at the transfusion place and eating
was a good way to kill time there. After I took Gary to
his porch to get a book, Mom and I moved him into the
front seat of the station wagon and then folded up the
wheelchair and put it in the back. The clinic was in a different building from Gary's doctor's office. They were
both in the city, and it took forty-five minutes to get
there.

I wheeled Gary into the modern clinic building,
pushing the chair over the purple carpet with the blue
crisscross pattern on it, past the textured cement walls.
All the pictures on the walls were views of the outdoors. And it struck me then that every doctor's office,
every hospital clinic, every medical place we had ever
been in, had only pictures showing the outdoors—gar-

dens, views from balconies, seascapes. It made me think of what Lisa had said about dying people liking to be outside, and Gary's need to go to the garden, and sleep on the screened porch.

The transfusion section was on the first floor, and we didn't have to wait at reception because they knew us, and anyway we were already a little bit late for Gary's appointment. We went past the desk into the main room, where there were big, soft recliner chairs. The nurse who always took care of Gary was named Janice. She had a long, sort of horsy face, but she was very kind and really seemed to care about Gary. The male nurses moved Gary easily over onto a recliner chair.

Janice also knew how to stick the IV needle into Gary's wrist in a way that didn't make him wince, the way he had done when other people had put lines in him earlier in his illness. She hung the plastic bag of blood up on the hook above Gary's chair. I had asked Janice before, when Mom wasn't around, why Gary needed new blood. What was wrong with his own blood? She said it would be better if I discussed that with my parents, and she was firm about it.

I didn't like to look at her inserting the needle, and looked at the book Gary had in his lap instead. It was called *The Basic Principles of Quantum Physics*. Maybe I would learn something after all—if Mom didn't hang around. The transfusion took at least an hour.

I went and got sandwiches and drinks from the cart. Gary had ham and cheese with six plastic packs of mustard and Mom and I had tuna. "Sure you don't want two sandwiches?" Mom said. "How about some chips? And maybe you should be drinking milk instead of soda, and not eating all that mustard."

"I'm the one who's going through this transfusion crap and it's not all that fun and I deserve to eat what I want," Gary said, and Mom knew there was no arguing with him. "You have any shopping to do or anything?" he asked her, when she was finishing her sandwich.

"Well, actually . . . Will you two be all right here?"

"I have my book," Gary said. "And there's plenty of magazines for Suze to read—unless she wants to go with you."

"No. I'll stay here with Gary," I said. Maybe he would tell me more about quantum. And even if he didn't, there was always the chance I could eavesdrop and learn something about his illness. Mom bustled out.

A man and a woman in the very next section were talking to a doctor, and they hadn't drawn the pink plastic curtain between them and us. I clearly heard the man say to the doctor, "Thank you, Sam, but I just can't help it. I know it's wonderful that the treatment took, but I just keep worrying the lymphoma will come back again."

"You're fine," the doctor assured him. "It isn't coming back. Just stop worrying and enjoy your house on the beach."

Had Gary heard that? I hoped not. I was furious at this man who had been cured, sitting right next to my brother who was probably dying, and talking about how worried he was, when he had nothing to worry about and Gary did. I seemed to care about Gary more than I'd realized.

I also wondered if what Gary had was lymphoma. Now I quickly said, so he wouldn't hear any more, "I see you brought one of your quantum books. Now that Mom isn't here, can you tell me more about it—and the garden?"

When Gary was being transfused, he got into a mood sort of like the one he got into at the pond. Maybe it was the recliner, maybe it was the feeling of the new, healthy blood being pumped into him. But he was generally less ornery and easier to talk to when the line was in him. You'd think it would be the other way, but there it was. So I hoped he might tell me something.

"Well, quantum physics is basically about a cat," he said.

"A cat? What does a cat have to do with anything?"

"You have to understand. This is really hard stuff. I

barely understand it myself and I'll probably be telling you some wrong things. But a cat is a very important part of it. And in a certain sense, I *am* that cat."

I sighed. "You're not making sense."

"You have to be patient and take it step by step. The cat is called Schrödinger's cat, after a German scientist from the first part of the twentieth century. Does that ring any kind of a bell to you? The name Schrödinger, and a cat?"

It did, but I wasn't sure why. And then it hit me. "Luke's cat. Sro-dee. The name is sort of the same."

"Yes. Kind of an amazing coincidence, because of Luke's connection with the quantum garden."

"So tell me," I prodded him, "what does this cat have to do with anything?"

"In the quantum world, which consists of the tiniest objects there are, the roots of everything, things are different from what we experience. What happens is controlled by probabilities, not definites. Like that bird this morning was a probability—it could have been in one place or another place. The same is true of radiation, which means an atom coming out of piece of radioactive matter—there's a fifty-fifty chance that the atom will come out in a certain time, and a fifty-fifty chance that it won't come out. You with me so far?" And he almost sort of smiled.

"Yeah. So far it makes sense."

"Well, so this guy Schrödinger set up a thought experiment. He imagined putting a live cat inside a box. There's also a little bottle of poison in the box, and a piece of radioactive matter. It's set up so that if an atom comes out of the radioactive matter, it will break the bottle and release the poison and the cat will die. If no atom comes out, the poison won't be released and the cat will live. There's no way of knowing. So it's like the cat is dead and alive at the same time. It's called uncertainty. Whether the cat is alive or dead is uncertain—until you open the box and look. And I'm that cat."

"You're telling me you're alive and dead at the same time?" It just popped out of me—it was such a strange thing for him to say.

Gary nodded. "That's one way of looking at it." His cheeks were not shining like earlier today; he was very pale. I saw now how scared he was—usually he covered it up. Maybe being scared was also part of his transfusion personality. He wanted to prove he didn't mind being transfused, but I could see through it.

I wanted to change the subject away from his condition. "But what does this Sro-dee cat have to do with the garden acting so peculiar?"

"I told you it was complicated," he said gently.

"Just tell me why the garden is like this quantum world—this uncertainty world."

"How can I explain?" He stared off into space for a moment. "Okay. In our big, slow world—or it would be better to say the way we *experience* the world—we know that if you kick a ball, it moves." And I couldn't help wondering if he would ever kick a ball again. "And if you have the right equipment, you can measure exactly where the ball is and exactly how fast it's going. You can understand that, right?"

"Yes, I can understand it." Now I was getting a little irritable at his teacher act.

"And in the big, slower cosmic world it's the same way—you know how fast the earth is moving around the sun, you know where it is, you know how fast a rocket is moving, you know where it is. You got that?"

"Just get to the point." I looked at my watch. Half an hour had gone by already; Mom would be back soon, and then we'd have to stop talking about this. And I *had* to understand how it related to what was happening in the garden.

"But deep down in the quantum world, among the tiniest particles of matter, which are the basis of everything there is, you *can't* know. You just can't. If you know how fast an electron is moving, you can't know where it is. And if you know where it is, then you can't know how fast it's going. It's the same uncertainty. It's complete craziness. The basic matter of the world is complete craziness."

"Just checking," Janice said, and came over and looked at the different gauges on Gary's transfusion pole. She smiled. "Everything okay?"

"Fine," Gary said. "Everything's fine."

"I'm very happy to hear it," Janice said, and went to check on another patient.

"Anyway all of life, all of the universe, is governed by this uncertainty, this craziness. It's just hidden from us up here—and it's faster than we can imagine." Gary was leaning forward, his wiry muscles tense. "Great-Uncle Arthur was part of this research that proved uncertainty. Great-Uncle Arthur made the garden. And now the uncertainty of the quantum world is getting big in there. It's taking over the garden. You can't know exactly where the bird is—it's in a lot of different places, a cloud of probabilities. And the bird can leak out of the porch. You can't know where the path is going to go. You can't know what different flowers are going to come up, or where, or when. And it's getting stronger. And I don't understand why it's happening now, when I'm like this. Almost as if Great-Uncle Arthur knew this was going to happen to me. And maybe this"—he lifted his hand with the needle in it, to indicate his illness without saying it directly—"triggered the uncertainty in the garden. Luke says what's happening in the garden is bad for me, but I'm not sure he's right."

"Do you think Luke knows about the cat that's alive and dead at the same time? Is that why he named his cat Sro-dee?"

Gary shrugged. "I have no idea. The only thing I know about Luke is that he's smart and he'll never tell."

"But . . . if the garden is being taken over by complete craziness, then maybe Luke is right that it's dangerous. You say that everything is uncertain. Does that mean that a tree could just suddenly fall down on you or something?"

Gary nodded eagerly, a trace of color coming back to his cheeks. "Yeah, it can be dangerous. And that's what makes it exciting. And maybe that's why it will make me get better. You never get anywhere if you don't take risks."

"I wonder if quantum had anything to do with Dad's aunt Caroline drowning in the pond?" I said.

Gary shrugged. "Maybe. Except that happened way before the quantum started to get big in there."

I knew more about quantum now, but it just made me more afraid of the garden than ever. And Gary had admitted that a tree *could* just fall down on you without warning. And I was going to have to take him there every morning?

"The uncertainty thing—it's like being a doctor. Or a patient." That part was hard for Gary to say, to admit, and he looked away from me. "A lot of doctors are good, they try hard. But there is so much they just can't know—medicine is still in its infancy." And I thought of the doctor in the next section—they had left, thank God—telling the man his lymphoma would never come back. Did he really know that? "And if you magnify that not knowing by a billion billion times, then you have the quantum world—the world that's taking over the garden, and getting stronger every day." And I could tell that even though we had been out there a long time this morning, Gary was already eager to go back.

"But I still don't see how a cat can be alive and dead at the same time," I said. What I really meant was that I couldn't see how Gary could be alive and dead at the same time.

"Well, that's only one interpretation. I didn't want to get too complicated at first. There's also Everett's version. He's another quantum physicist." He was sitting up now, more excited. "In his version, the cat lives *and* dies."

I shook my head. "I don't get it."

"Both events happen. The particle comes out of the

radioactive matter and breaks the bottle and the poison is released and the cat dies. And the particle also *doesn't* come out, and the cat lives. And when that happens, the universe splits, it bifurcates. And now there are two universes, one in which the cat dies, and one in which it lives." He picked up the book. "This is *real science*. They proved it experimentally. There are an infinite number of universes. They branch off randomly, like limbs on a tree. And—"

And there was Mom, and Janice, arriving both at the same time. Just when it was getting really interesting. "How is he doing?" Mom asked her.

And I could see what Gary meant about uncertainty. "I've taken all his signs," Janice said gently, as she removed the empty, clear plastic red-stained, squashed bag from the pole. "They're in the computer. The doctor will look at them and let you know." It was exactly the same thing she said every time Mom asked exactly the same question. And there never seemed to be any certain answers.

There was a phone message for me from Lisa when we got home. "Maybe I could come over tomorrow morning when you go out with Gary," Lisa said. "And I could help you."

I sat there and thought before calling her back. If she

had said anything about the maze, the answer would have been a definite no. But she wisely hadn't mentioned the maze—and I doubted it was because she had lost interest in it. She was smart enough to know it would put me off. My fear was that she would mention it to Gary, and then he would get all gung ho about it.

I was also uncomfortable about the fact that Lisa already knew about quantum—we would certainly be talking about it again after today. On the other hand, I had already learned something—and maybe Gary would let me look at some of his books for the rest of the afternoon, and fill me in a little more.

And if Lisa was with us, then there would be one other person who would be a witness to what was going on. For some reason Gary didn't want Mom and Dad to know about the garden—maybe he was afraid that if they knew, it would somehow keep the garden from curing him. Luke had said he had to think about the path, alone, maybe praying to his God. And I had to admit it was hard for me to imagine Luke talking to Dad or Mom about the path moving.

But Lisa was different. She *would* talk to them. She was blunt. Dad might not be able to fend her off. And even though I didn't like the idea of her understanding quantum better than me, she might help *me* understand it better.

But before I called her back I talked to Gary about it. "Can you trust her?" he said, reclining with his books on a pile of pillows on his bed.

"Trust her?" I said, not understanding.

"I don't want a lot of people to know about the garden. The less people who know, the better. People might be afraid it could spread. They could try to stop it."

"Lisa thinks the garden is cool," I told him. "She wouldn't say a word if we told her not to."

"Then tell her to come," he said, turning a page. "It might be a good change."

This annoyed me. It was like he was saying she would be more interesting than just me. But *I* also thought it would be a good change—her presence might make Gary less bossy. And so I called her and invited her to come at nine the next day.

And the three of us would go into the garden together for the first time.

"But don't say anything to Gary about the maze," I told her.

"Why not?"

It was just like her to argue about it. "Because I'm not ready for it yet. I don't want Gary to get it into his head. The quantum will be stronger there. It only makes sense. It could hurt him. The garden is already dangerous enough."

"Quantum?" Lisa said curiously. "You said something about that before."

"It's a quantum garden, Lisa. It was planned that way. Our Great-Uncle Arthur won the Lebon Prize for quantum physics and he was a big part of making the garden. That's what's so dangerous about it."

"Then you'll be safer if I'm there to help," she said. "See you at nine tomorrow."

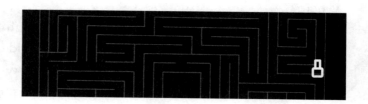

Lisa was over a few minutes after nine.

We had eaten breakfast—again, Gary had two eggs and two pieces of toast—and I was asking him questions on his porch.

"Okay, I guess I can accept about the cat dying and the cat staying alive, and how that makes two universes, one with a dead cat and one with a live cat." I thought of Gary, and which alternative would happen to him in this universe, but I didn't mention it—it would get things off to a bad start. "But you also said there are *infinite* universes. That's kind of hard to believe, even though you said they proved it. Why do there have to be infinite ones?"

He sighed. "I'm not sure exactly how to explain it. It's like, there are all these interactions going on in the quantum world. And every time one thing happens instead of another thing, then—"

The doorbell rang. I stood up. "Should I bring her in here?"

He shrugged, acting like he didn't care, though I was sure he was very glad to be seeing another kid—and probably soon showing off all his scientific knowledge. "Sure. Why not?" he said. "As long as you're sure we can trust her."

"Come on out to the porch," I said to Lisa at the door. "We're talking about some weird stuff." I didn't mention that part of my reason for asking Gary all these questions was to put off going into the garden for as long as possible. Gary was so eager. I had my reasons not to be.

"Do you know about Schrödinger's cat?" was the first thing Gary said to Lisa when he saw her.

"Hey, yeah," she said coolly. "I was going to ask you about that. It sounds weird, but—Susan said the garden acts the way it does because it's a quantum garden."

"Do you know that Luke's cat is named Sro-dee?" Gary said.

"As in Schrödinger," she said like a student in class. "Does that mean Luke's part of the quantum stuff, too?"

"I don't know," Gary said. "But here's what I do know. Not one word of any of this is leaving this house and this garden. You got that? Unless you swear the strongest oath not to tell a *single person* about what's going on in this garden, you're leaving now. Do you understand? Did you tell anybody yet?"

"I told my parents about the lotuses and the other flowers. They didn't take it seriously."

"That's good," Gary said. He gave me a hard look. "We're lucky she didn't spread it around. From now on you are not to tell *anybody* about any of this. You got that? If people find out what's really going on, they'll try to stop it. They'll mow the garden to the ground." He turned to Lisa. "You don't want that to happen, do you?"

Lisa put her hand to her mouth and blankly shook her head. "No," she said. "I think the garden is really cool."

"I hope so," Gary said. "Are you religious? Like, can you swear an oath to God?"

Lisa squeezed her fingers tightly together. "I can swear an oath to every God anybody ever believed in in the history of the world. I swear it! I swear it now and forever!" Her voice was so fervent that she sounded like she could burst into tears at any minute.

Even Gary was convinced. "Okay. Let's get rolling,"

he said. "Hey, you don't even know about the bird."

He had to let Lisa help me move him into the wheel-chair. Either he was getting heavier, or Lisa wasn't as strong as Dad. I suspected the latter. As I rolled him through the living room, I noticed Lisa glancing toward the stairway—the stairway that led to the bathroom with the only window in the house from which you could see the maze. I wished I'd made her swear an oath not to say anything about the maze to Gary.

"The bird?" she said to Gary.

"There was a probability bird on my porch yesterday morning. I'll tell you later. I've got to find out something else first."

Down the ramp, across the lawn, through the orchard, over to Luke's shed.

"Knock on the door, Susan. I hope he's still here. I want to clear something up."

I knocked. "Yes?" came Luke's voice from inside.

"It's Gary and Susan and Lisa," I said. "Can . . . we talk to you for a minute?"

"Just a moment please," he said. We waited. When Luke unlocked and opened the door I could smell the sickly sweet, smoky aroma of incense, and you could see its smoke in the light from the small window. He must have been praying. I had never smelled the incense before. Was he praying more now because of what was happening to the garden? "Hello. Good morning," he said. "I'm happy to see you again, Lisa."

Sro-dee was perched on his shoulder. "Good morning, Luke," Gary said. "Good morning, Sro-dee." Sro-dee leaped down onto Gary's lap, as though he understood that Gary had greeted him. Gary was obviously pleased, holding and stroking him, and Sro-dee stretched and purred, enjoying it, too.

Then Gary looked Luke straight in the eye. "Is there any special reason why you named him Sro-dee?" Gary asked him.

Luke paused. Then he said, "Now I tell you a true thing. I do not name him. When I first come to work here, cat is already here, a tiny baby. Susan only little girl. Old man still alive then. He tell me name of cat is Sro-dee. Not Cambodian name." He looked away. "Only Cambodian word like it is srool. Means fun."

Gary watched him coolly, assessing him. "So there was still an old man here when you came," he said finally. "Was it Great-Uncle Arthur?"

"Don't remember."

"He tell you anything about the garden—anything special about it?"

Luke shrugged uncomfortably. "No." It was hard to tell whether to believe him or not. "He say he knows too much work for one person, just do the best I can.

And now I have to do the best I can and have to go right away." He picked up Sro-dee and put him on his shoulder. I somehow sensed that Gary and Sro-dee did not want to be separated. Luke went into the shed and came out with a trowel and a shovel. He went and stood directly in front of Gary's chair. "Don't go on path today. Don't go on path anymore. I don't like story of bird and lotus. Not safe for you."

I felt a powerful surge of relief. How wonderful not to have to go into the woods any more!

"Yeah, but wait," Gary said. "You didn't—"

Luke turned and strolled away, off behind the outhouse. And then I saw that most of the red flowers had been cut down. Only Luke could have done it. Was he afraid?

"Can't get much of anything out of him. As usual," Gary said. "But Sro-dee doesn't seem that old that he would have already been here when Susan was a baby."

"Maybe the garden kept him young—and killed off all your other relatives," Lisa said. "Maybe the garden likes him because of Schrödinger's cat."

"Could be," Gary said, as though it made sense—he rarely admitted that anything I said made sense. "Well, come on. Let's get going."

"Going where?" I said, apprehensive.

"To the path, of course. Where else does anything

happen?"

"But Luke said not to go on the path anymore."

"Luke isn't my boss. Luke doesn't have to know. Did you smell the incense? He's superstitious, that's all. *You* want to go on the path and see what happened to the lotuses, right, Lisa?"

I turned and looked at her. If Lisa was anybody else, she would have been in a predicament. Technically, I was her friend. I had brought her here in the first place. That meant she should be on my side. But I knew she wanted to go to the pond. And Lisa said what she wanted. "Did you ever notice the cool mushrooms on that path?" she said to Gary. "Amanitas."

"Amanitas? Wow! I've never seen one. Come on, Susan. What are you waiting for?"

"But Luke said it was dangerous. *You* said it was dangerous. A tree could fall down on us for no reason. Anything could happen."

"You stay. I'll push the chair," Lisa said coolly.

I felt angry and betrayed. But I wasn't going to let her have the chair. Anyway, she'd have problems with it— she was smaller and not as strong as I had come to be. "Okay," I said, and took a few slow, deep breaths. "But if anything crazy starts to happen, I'm getting out of there and I don't care what either of you say."

In the darkness under the trees, Gary spotted an

Amanita before Lisa did. "Why didn't I notice it before? You have good eyes," he complimented her.

"It's way bigger than the ones I saw the other day," she said. It was about the size of a small fist, red with white dots. "It could probably kill two or three people, easy."

I wanted to keep moving and get this over with, but they were enthralled and kept studying the ugly thing. And the next one we came to was even bigger, and they studied it even more. It took forever to get to the bridge. It was a good thing it was a sunny day and still relatively early in the morning. How long would they want to dawdle in here anyway?

I could hear the pine needles whispering in the wind. I wasn't afraid of something jumping out at me anymore. I was afraid of a tree falling on me. It could happen at any second. This was quantum land. Everything was uncertain.

"Oh! You were going to tell me about a bird," Lisa reminded Gary. They were talking to each other and almost completely ignoring me. I was the chair pusher.

But for some reason I didn't completely understand, I *wanted* to be the chair pusher. It must have been the control thing again—even though they were really controlling me by making me go deeper into this place. But with the chair in my hands, I could always get us out of here fast—to wherever the path decided to take us.

Gary reminded Lisa of Luke's folktale, and then told her about how the probability bird had come out of the lotus the next morning. She caught on pretty fast, of course. "Wish I'd been there to actually see it," she said.

"It was amazing," said Gary.

"And scary," I added. "You were scared, too, Gary. You were cringing away from it. It was everywhere and nowhere at the same time."

"All right, all right." Gary looked at his watch, then craned forward. "We ought to be reaching the pond soon. Where is it?"

"Maybe there's so many lotuses there's no pond anymore," I said, and explained to Lisa how fast the lotuses had proliferated since the last time we had been there. Then I looked down the path. "There's light up ahead. There shouldn't be . . . Maybe we should turn around and go back."

"Keep going!" Gary and Lisa said in one voice.

Why had I ever asked her over here? Without her, Gary might have paid more attention to Luke's warnings. Neither of them would be satisfied until we got to the pond.

But the pond kept not being there. The trees thinned. The path was taking us to different places in *both* directions now. I could only keep pushing. Would we ever get home again?

And then I saw it: the first hedge of the maze.

It was wild and unkempt, of course. How could Luke find it to trim it? Not that I had ever really believed it existed except from that one bathroom window.

Lisa couldn't control herself. "The maze!" she shouted. "Sorry, Susan. But how can I not mention it when we're actually here? Except . . ." And then she folded her hands together and looked from side to side. "You said you'd never been to the maze. And last time I was on this path it went to the pond. The path never came here before, did it? I didn't believe you, Susan, but now I've *seen* it. The garden is getting *completely* out of control now, isn't it?" Finally she was wisening up and getting scared. "How . . . how are we ever going to get back?"

Gary was sitting up straight in his chair, his cheeks glowing. "I never thought I'd get here in my life." He bounced in his chair, more energetic than he'd been in a long time. I could feel his weight pushing against the handles. "Oh! Come on, come on, let's go."

"But what if we never get *out*?" I asked him. "Regular, normal mazes are designed for you to get lost in. A maze on this path—where on earth would it take us?"

"That's what I want to know," Gary said, breathing hard.

"Well, maybe we could just get a little bit closer to it, without actually going in," Lisa said, taking his side, of course.

I could always turn around and go back. I was in control of the chair. But would it make any difference? The path was unpredictable in both directions now. What was the difference between going forward and going back?

And part of me was curious, too. Just to see the beginning of the maze. And then we could turn around and go back over the bridge and get closer to home.

I pushed the chair forward.

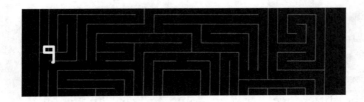

9

The trees ended abruptly. What had been here to keep them from growing into the maze?

The entrance to the maze was two hedges, about five feet apart. They were several feet taller than me and very thick and bushy—there was clearly no way to see over or through them. The ground between them was covered with gravel, or else the grass would have been so high it would have been tough going even without the chair.

About fifteen feet ahead, the hedge path split at right angles, making a T intersection.

We just stood there. Even Gary didn't say anything. If we went in, would we ever—ever in our lives—get back to the path in the woods? We didn't know where the path in the woods would take us, but so far it had always taken us someplace recognizable, from which we could get home.

That wasn't true of the maze. You could only see it from one window in the house. I was sure it would take us to someplace we'd have a harder time finding our way back from.

"We could just go as far as the intersection and look down both paths to see where they go—but not get out of sight of the entrance," Gary suggested.

Lisa and I looked at each other, and I sensed we were both having the same thought: Once we got to the intersection, would we even be able to *see* where the entrance had been?

"I have an idea," Lisa said, still sounding scared. "I'll wait here and not take my eyes off you. Then whatever happens you'll be able to get back to the entrance."

"Good idea," Gary said. "Come on. Let's go."

I wasn't so sure. We were in the heart of quantum territory now. Things would be even crazier here. "Well . . ." I said.

"Susan, it's only fifteen feet. I promise I won't try to make you turn the corner. You can even pull me backward and keep your eyes on Lisa all the time."

With a deep feeling of dread, I turned the chair around and began pulling it backward toward the intersection, turning around and looking where I was going, then turning back to check on Lisa. The gravel path was crackly and easier going than the path in the woods.

And after about five feet Lisa began to change. She blurred. There wasn't just one Lisa. There was a cloud of Lisas.

I stopped, staring at her. "She's getting like the bird," I said to Gary. "We don't know where she is exactly anymore. She's an uncertainty." There was a chance she was in one particular place, but only a chance. I looked away from her and down at my hands. There were eight of them, all blurred together—and Gary's eight heads were blurred together, too. I screamed. "Look at *us*!"

"Yes, but Lisa's still in that area. And so are we. And she's not crazy afraid like the bird; she's not going to run away. Only a few more feet. We take a look. We go back."

I started moving back again. The Lisas and Garys spread out as their probability clouds got bigger and bigger. The farther we went, the less likely she was to be in any particular place, and us too. And we were all turning transparent.

But we had reached the intersection and the Lisa cloud was still at the entrance. We looked down the path in both directions.

There were no more right angles. Paths veered off in

every direction. Only three feet in there and you'd have no idea how to get back.

And Lisa was vaguer than ever. I was terrified she was going to disappear altogether. "Okay, you had your look. We're going back," I said, and pushed the chair running back toward the fading cloud of Lisas.

And the closer we got, the more solid we all became. I thanked the maze and the garden for not making us disappear. By the time we got back to her, she was one person, solid and normal—if you could call Lisa normal.

"Wow . . . ," she breathed.

"It looked the same way to you as it did to us?" Gary asked her. "You saw us turn into a probability cloud?"

She nodded, pale, unable to speak for a moment. "I was afraid . . . you were going to disappear completely," she said. "Can we . . . try to go back now?"

Even Gary seemed to have had enough for one day. "Okay, okay. Let's see where the path takes us today."

We crossed the wooden bridge. I braced myself as we reached the edge of the woods. "Last time it dumped us in the valley," I told Lisa. "If it does that, I'll need your help fast to pull the chair back up the hill."

She nodded, biting her lip.

I carefully pushed the chair out of the trees.

We were in the meadow, in exactly the same place

where we had always entered the path.

Gary laughed, in a strained way. "I guess it figured it did enough weird stuff for one day," he said.

"*I've* had enough weird stuff for one day," Lisa said. "Can we go back now?" And, to my surprise, Gary agreed.

Lisa stayed for a while and looked through some of Gary's quantum books. But she seemed edgy. She left before lunch. Now I was afraid she had been scared away and might never come back again. And now I *wanted* her to come back. We were going to end up in the maze again; Gary would badger me to death if I didn't take him. And the maze would be worse if Lisa wasn't there.

The adventure in the maze didn't seem to have exhausted Gary as I would have expected. To Mom's delight, he had one and a half sandwiches for lunch. He didn't lie down on his bed as he usually did in the afternoons—he sat in the chair at his desk on the porch and read his quantum and his garden books. At supper that night Dad and I hardly had to lift him at all, his legs did so much of the work. And he had two big helpings of macaroni and cheese.

"The maze," Gary said, when he and I were alone on the porch before he went to sleep. "It . . . made me stronger."

I didn't want to believe it. I couldn't stand to believe it. The maze was the most terrifying place I could ever imagine.

And yet it really did seem to be good for him.

Then I noticed. The lotus, closed now, was in a different vase, not the Chinese one but a solid blue ceramic one I had never seen before. "Did you put the lotus in a different vase, Gary?" I asked him.

"No," he said, looking at it with surprise. "I never moved it from that Chinese dragon one."

"Let me check," I said. I went back to the kitchen. There was no Chinese vase there. I asked Mom where it was, but she didn't remember it. It didn't seem to exist anymore.

"There is no Chinese vase," I told Gary, shivering a little.

"I don't get it," he said, and yawned. By now he was tired.

The next morning was his doctor's appointment. The nurse took his blood and we waited while they ran it through all the tests, and compared it with the tests Janice had taken the other day. Then we were ushered into the doctor's office.

He was all smiles. "The transfusion the other day must have helped a lot," he said. "All your counts are improved, Gary. It's always hard to know what to do in these situations, it's always uncertain. But maybe we finally hit on the right combination of medications." He shook his head, still smiling. "I'm not sure I've ever seen such a dramatic change in blood counts."

The doctor was nicer than he had ever been, because he thought he had done something very smart.

Gary and I just looked at each other. We knew it wasn't the medications that were making him stronger. They never had before. It was the garden—and especially the maze.

"And maybe something else even weirder," Gary said to me as I wheeled him out of the hospital.

"Something weirder?" Mom asked. We hadn't realized she'd been so close, eavesdropping. It wasn't like her to do that.

"Nothing," Gary said.

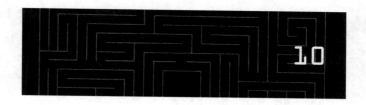

10

It started raining on the way back from the doctor's, so we wouldn't have to go out that afternoon. That was a relief.

At home, after lunch, when Mom had finally left us and Gary and I were back on the porch, he said, "You better call that friend of yours and warn her again."

"You mean Lisa? Warn her about what?"

"Okay, she thought the garden was cool—at first. But the maze really threw her. I could feel it, I could see it. Couldn't you?"

I nodded. "Yeah. When the path moved, and especially after we all turned into probabilities, she changed," I agreed. "She just wanted to get out of the garden, she just wanted to get home. She might never come back here again after that. And somehow I'd . . .

well, I'd kind of like it if she *did* come back."

"That's not the point," Gary said. "The point is that if she's really scared, she might run to Mommy and Daddy. She probably wouldn't try to tell them the truth—she already knows they'd never believe it. But her parents will see that she's really scared, if anybody will. And they won't like it. They may try to interfere. She's got to act like nothing unusual happened here, nothing that scared her."

"You think she can pull it off?" I said doubtfully. Lisa didn't cover up her emotions, like most people did.

Gary slapped the arm of his chair, breathing hard. "You heard what the doctor said, you see the way I'm eating now. That place is saving my life. We've got to prevent even the *slightest* chance that something could interfere with it. She's that chance. It would have been better if she'd never seen it. You brought her here. Now you make sure she doesn't give anything away."

"But she swore she wouldn't tell," I said, somehow reluctant to make this call.

"That's not enough." Gary was really vehement about this. "Tell her anything that will keep her quiet. Tell her the truth—that the garden, and the maze, are making me better. If she has any . . . any *atom* of decency in her, that should keep her quiet."

I sighed. But he was right. I had to do it.

There was no phone on the porch so I went up to my room and called her.

"Hi. How's it going?" Lisa said, sounding a little hesitant. Her voice dropped. "Did you go back to . . . the maze?"

"No. We went to Gary's doctor, before it started to rain. And . . . he's getting better. The doctor says it's the medications, but we think it's the garden—and the maze."

"Well, that's great that he's getting better, but not great about the maze," Lisa said. "Does it mean you'll have to keep going back there?"

I noticed immediately that she didn't include herself in the maze expeditions.

"Listen, Lisa, this is important. You swore you wouldn't tell anybody about the garden or the maze. You have to keep your promise. I know it was scary, but . . . it really is making Gary better. The doctor said he'd never seen anything like it. But if your parents got the idea there was something really dangerous here, they might try to do something about it. Something more than just not letting you come here. They might tell somebody, maybe even the police. They would destroy the garden and that would be the end of it. Gary would stop getting better."

"That garden's dangerous," she said, not sounding

convinced. "I thought it was cool at first, but now . . ."

"Lisa, I trusted you. You never have to go to the maze again. But please, please don't tell anybody. Think of Gary. He could die.

"And maybe . . . you could come over again tomorrow. We won't go to the maze," I lied. I knew Gary would want to go there—he had only missed today because of the doctor and the rain. "Anyway, we have no way of knowing if the path will take us there. Just drop by after breakfast."

"Okay." But she sure didn't sound as enthusiastic as she had been before we'd been to the maze—and she was on the one who'd been so fascinated by it at first.

"You were looking at Gary's books yesterday. Did you read about the other universes?" I asked her. "Like how every time there's a tiny quantum change, the universe splits? The word they use is bifurcate."

"Yeah. I saw a diagram. There's millions of quantum changes all the time. And millions of universes."

"Well, Gary thinks maybe that has something to do with the maze."

"*Really?*" Her voice perked up. At least she was still a little bit weird. "Okay. Maybe we can just *look* at the maze again. See you tomorrow. Hope the weather's better than today."

Maybe she would come after all. I didn't know what

Lisa could do to make us safer in the maze, but it just felt better to have somebody else around.

"I tell you not to go on the path," Luke said the next morning, as we were heading straight for it.

Sro-dee jumped off his shoulder onto Gary's lap, which gave Gary the chance to ignore Luke's admonition and cuddle with the cat. "Well we did go—the day before yesterday. And it didn't take us to the pond. It took us to the maze." He looked up and met Luke's eyes. "Do you know about the maze, Luke?" He was sitting up straighter than when he had first started using the chair.

Luke, whose expression was usually so cheerful, looked stricken. "You mean—the place with all the paths and the tall hedges that go around and around?" he said, actually sounding scared.

"Yes. Have you ever been there?"

"The old man—he tell me about it."

"I'm really curious about this old man who named Sro-dee after Schrödinger's cat," Gary said, lifting up the cat to look it in the eye. His arms were stronger now. "This man who just disappeared, like all our relatives. The only one we really know what happened to is Dad's aunt Caroline. Dad said all the others went to other countries and died, but we never visited them, and there were never any funerals. It must have been Great-Uncle Arthur, the quantum scientist, who named the cat. What did he tell you about the maze, about the garden, about everything?"

Luke looked down, his arms behind his back. "He tell me very little. Almost nothing."

"But he told you *something*. And listen, Luke. Since the maze I'm a lot stronger. And the doctor said I was doing much better—my blood is getting better now, not worse, like before. He said he'd never seen anything like it. The path and the maze can't be all bad if they're doing that to me. That's why I want to know what the old man said. Everything."

Luke's shoulders sagged, and he looked older than I had ever seen him. He had always looked young before, but now suddenly he seemed middle-aged. "Hard to remember, because so long ago, and I was so young. But I think . . ." He sighed. "I think he said it is the heart of the garden, where all the strange things that are going to happen someday are going to come from." He brightened a little, and quickly changed the subject from what the old man had said. "But you say you go in there and you get better? And doctor say you are better, too?"

"Yes," Gary insisted, folding his arms.

"We only went a little way," I said. "Lisa stayed outside so we wouldn't get lost, and we didn't go far enough to turn any corners. Want to come with us this time?" I asked him. "I mean, if the path even takes us there. And we can explain what it means. It's very scientific."

Luke lifted his hands. "So much work to do around here, and no time. I can't just go off for no reason to see this place." He stood up straighter. "And I don't want you to go there again."

"Just once," Gary pleaded. "It's making me better. I think that's what the old man made it for."

"Well . . ." Luke watched Gary's face with a strange expression, then looked away. He sighed. Then he spoke very hesitantly. "Quickly, then," Luke finally agreed. "Only because of what doctor say."

We stepped into the darkness under the trees, walking as fast as we could. I wasn't sure why we wanted Luke to see the maze and the people turning into probability clouds, but for some reason Gary and I did, and I was sure Lisa did, too—though she seemed strangely sullen.

Were we going to go deeper into the maze today? With more people there, we could make a sort of chain, so that we could go farther but still always have somebody in sight to lead us back.

But not too far.

It was a while since we had crossed the bridge, and there was no evidence of the pond. Luke was moving very stealthily, as if he knew that something could fall on us at any second. How much *had* "the old man" told him? How much did he know that he wasn't telling us?

And then the brightness ahead, and the trees stopping. We were heading for the maze all right. Lisa was behind Luke now, walking more slowly. Gary and I were in the lead. Sro-dee was still in Gary's lap, but not curled up and cuddly. He was standing on all fours, alert, his nose twitching. We stopped where we could see the two entrance hedges, but didn't get too close to them.

"Okay, here's the plan," Gary said, full of confidence, as if he didn't expect anyone to disagree with him. "Lisa stays just where she did the last time, just inside, so we can always see the entrance. Luke comes with us to the first branching, and stays there, so we can always find him. And Susan and I take the left path or the right path—but we don't lose sight of Luke. But if we should . . . Sro-dee will lead us to him." He picked Sro-dee up and looked him in the eye again, as if he thought the cat could really understand him.

He put the cat back down again, and he *did* seem to understand because he didn't try to get back onto Luke's shoulder. "Luke, have you been here before or haven't you? Because if you haven't, we have to explain what's going to happen."

Luke's gaze shifted back and forth, as if he didn't know what to say. We somehow knew that he wouldn't lie. But he might avoid telling the truth. He sighed. "He took me here once. He know another way—the path didn't move then. He said he hide it, so nobody come here—but could not hide completely."

He paused, as if he didn't want to talk about it, then went on reluctantly. "He make me stand just inside the maze and he does the same thing you do—he walk to where the path goes apart. And it still scares me to think of it. He gets like bad TV picture. Fuzzy, like more than one of him." He put his hand to his forehead. "It hurt my eyes to see it. But he come right back. He says he can't explain to me why this happens." He turned to Gary. "And now you make me come back here, because you say it make you better. That's the only reason I come this far. But I don't like it. And I don't have time. We go back now."

Gary and I looked at each other. We both sensed even more strongly that Luke wasn't telling us everything.

"But Luke, why do you think Great-Uncle Arthur made the maze, if there wasn't some good reason for it?" Gary said. "Maybe it was to help me get better. And now I'm asking *you* to help—just for a very short time. Lisa will stand here. You stand at the first branch so we can see you, and we'll find out what happens when we go deeper in."

Luke didn't refuse.

Lisa was pale, but her mouth was set in a hard line. I began pushing the wheelchair into the maze, Sro-dee still in Gary's lap. Luke walked behind us. I didn't watch Lisa this time, I didn't want to see her turn into a probability cloud; it was bad enough seeing Gary's head and my own hands and the wheelchair start to blur, spreading slowly and in tiny increments out into copies of themselves. I could hear Luke whispering under his breath in what must have been Cambodian. Maybe he was praying.

We reached the T intersection. "Luke, you wait here. And please keep an eye on us."

"Which way?" I whispered, trying to keep my voice from shaking.

"Left, because I'm left-handed."

I turned left. Almost immediately I had to make another choice—a choice that would put Luke around a corner, making it impossible to see him.

"Gary, this is crazy," I said. The wheelchair had blurred to a cloud the size of a big car. "If I take one more step, we'll never find our way out."

"Luke!" Gary called out, turning to look behind him.

"Keep calling out, so we can hear you and find you."

"We must go back now," Luke said.

"I just want to go a little further," Gary said. "Keep calling my name, Luke." He paused for a moment. "Susan, take another left."

I took another left. And as I did, I saw another cloud of Susans and Garys go to the right.

"Wow!" Gary murmured in awe. "I bet if we kept coming here the place would be full of us."

"Gary!" we heard Luke calling behind us. "Susan! Bring him back *now*!"

And then I saw a cloud of us on a path ahead of me, deeper into the maze, a bigger, more diffuse cloud. The Susans were wearing denim cutoffs, not the black shorts I had on today. Gary's shoulders were thicker and straighter. The Susans looked really scared, their faces dead white. They were in a hurry; they were running away from something.

I was too terrified to be curious. I quickly turned around.

The path had branched behind us. Had it changed, or had I just not noticed the other turning? I didn't know which way to go. I could hear Luke calling, but it didn't help; both paths went in the direction of his voice.

And then Gary took Sro-dee off his lap and dropped him on the ground. Without hesitation the cat took one of the paths. "Follow the cat!" Gary shouted.

I took the path that Sro-dee did—and almost ran into the cloud of Lukes at the T intersection, Sro-dees already perched on his shoulder. The cloud of Lisas was still there ahead of us.

I pushed the chair fast and watched with relief as she became a single Lisa again.

"Enough," Luke said, and marched off down the path.

"I'm never coming here again," Lisa said, sounding angry, as though I had tricked her, which in a way I had.

But I couldn't worry about that now. I hurried after Luke. I knew I was stronger now, or else I wouldn't have been able to go this fast; but it was also harder to push the chair because Gary was heavier.

Would the path take us back to the right place again this time? If it didn't, I wanted Luke to be there.

And as I ran after him, I wondered who the other Garys and Susans I had seen had been. They had to be another version of us, on another day, deeper into the maze, because their clothes were different. If the maze could warp space and turn us into probability clouds, then why couldn't it warp time, too? And were they in the same universe, or a different one?

We crossed the bridge. "Luke, wait, I might need

your help!" I called out, and he did slow down a little bit.

And the path behaved itself again and took us to the right place in the meadow. It was as if it was rewarding us for going into the maze, as if it *wanted* us to go into the maze.

"I am cleaning my hands of this," Luke said as he walked off. "Do not ask me to come here again." And in a moment he was gone.

"Gary," I said, almost gasping. "You saw that other version of us, right? Deeper into the maze. More of a cloud than ever."

He shrugged. "Yeah, I saw," he said, as if the whole nightmare event had been nothing.

"There were other versions of you in there?" Lisa said.

"Yes. And we were wearing different clothes," Gary said. "We'll be back in there again."

"I'm going home. I don't want to know about it," Lisa said.

"I think it would be better for you if you came to the porch and did some studying," Gary said, watching her closely. "The more you know, the less scared and the safer you'll be."

"The more I never go back to that place, the safer I'll be."

"Well, I *have* to go there. And so does Susan. Whether you go or not."

I stifled a groan. If going into the maze was going to get him out of the wheelchair, then what choice did I have?

We looked at Gary's books, but we didn't find anything of much practical use. The people who wrote these books were talking about a world they never expected to see with their own eyes, let alone enter. There were no directions for how to get a probability cloud of electrons—let alone people—out of a quantum maze. There were descriptions of experiments about how if you shot an electron through one of two holes so that it would hit a screen and make an impression on it, it would look as though the single electron had gone through *both* holes. It said the path the electron took was completely unpredictable—that it could travel around the universe on its way to the screen. That was the quantum world. Gary thought it was all fascinating. But he'd been wrong when he said that learning any more would make us safer inside the maze.

And Lisa really had changed. She wasn't the least bit excited about the garden or the maze anymore. She was fidgety and almost silent. It was obvious she just wanted to get out of here. When Mom poked her head in and invited her for lunch, she said her mother was expecting her at home—she had afternoon chores to do.

"Lisa?" Gary entreated her, taking hold of her hand. "You want me to get better, don't you? That means you just can't tell anybody about any of this. Not your parents, not anybody."

She sighed and looked away from him. "Okay, okay," she said.

"Do you promise?" he went on.

"I promise," she said dully.

At the door I said to her, "Listen, Lisa. Don't think you have to go back in there."

"I already know I'm never going back in there," she said.

"Fine. *Just don't tell anybody about it.*"

She grabbed my hand and said, "But you're going to have to go back in there. And I don't think it's safe. I'm worried about you. I don't want you to do it."

"But what about Gary? Don't I have to help him get better?"

"I bet the doctor was right. They finally found the right medications. Why would going into that crazy, unreal place make him better? It doesn't make sense, Susan. Don't let Gary get you trapped away from the real world forever. Then your parents would lose you both. Use your head." And she left.

And now I was really worried. It wasn't that she just wasn't interested in the garden any more, or even just afraid of it. She sounded actively antagonistic toward it.

11

"I don't think Lisa's coming back," I said to Gary on the porch before supper.

"Fine. It's better if she stays away—she'll be less likely to tell. We don't need her anyway. All we need is the cat—the cat will know how to find the way back. That's why Great-Uncle Arthur named him Sro-dee."

"You mean—you want us to actually go all the way into that place—on our own?" In a way, I had known this was coming, but I could still hardly believe it.

"What else is there to do?" Gary said, sounding as reasonable as ever. "Every time I go in there, I get stronger. You want me out of this chair almost as much as I do, don't you? Then you won't have to spend all your time taking care of me."

"Yeah, but . . . but what if we get stuck in there and

never get out?"

"I told you, the cat knows the way."

"How are we going to get the cat away from Luke? He'll never let us take him if he knows we're going to bring him into the maze."

"There's got to be a way," Gary said thoughtfully. "I bet I can get Dad to help us—without him even realizing it." I wondered what he meant. But he didn't say any more.

I found out at supper.

When Dad and I started to carry Gary from the wheelchair into his chair at the table, we hardly had to lift him at all, his legs were so much stronger. "Good going, guy," Dad said.

It was a warm day, and Mom had made Salad Niçoise, French tuna salad, arranged on a platter with potato salad and green beans in olive oil and garlic, tomatoes, olives, and hard-boiled eggs. Gary was really shoveling it in, and the French bread, too.

"Is it my imagination, or are you eating more every day?" Dad asked him. "You sure look stronger. And you got out of the wheelchair almost completely on your own." He was beaming.

"It's because of the greenhouse," Gary said.

I almost dropped my fork, it was so unexpected. But of course I didn't say anything. Gary had a plan. And so far his plans about the garden, scary as they were, had worked.

"You know what the doctor said," Mom reminded him. "Gary's doing better because they finally got the medications right."

"I don't know anything about the medications," Gary said. "I just know that every day when I spend time at the greenhouse I feel better. And it's such a mess. Maybe you could ask Luke to do some work on it. Fix it up so there's not so much broken glass and stuff. Make it stronger. Clean it. Then it would be easier for me to spend time there and get even better. He could even grow some plants in it."

"But he has so much weeding to do," Mom said. "Isn't that more important? The greenhouse is a lost cause."

What was wrong with Mom, anyway? Gary fixed his eyes on her. "I said, *the greenhouse makes me stronger*," he said in a steely voice. "Are the weeds more important than that?"

"Well . . . er . . . ," Mom said.

Now I understood. If Luke was working in the greenhouse, he wouldn't want Sro-dee there, with all that glass and stuff. He'd be preoccupied and away from his shed. That would make it easier for Gary to take Sro-dee into the maze—since Luke had said he was never going back there again. I thought back. Had Sro-dee been with the other versions of us I had seen today? I couldn't remember.

"Well, why not?" Dad said. "We'd have to pay him extra, of course, for doing that kind of work. But if the greenhouse makes Gary stronger, what's more important than that?"

Dad knew more than anybody else about the garden. He must realize it had peculiar properties, though he would never admit it.

"Yes. I'm sorry. You're right, dear," Mom said, in a meek voice.

"Maybe you could ask him tonight," Gary said. "The sooner the better. I don't want to lose this . . . this energy, or whatever it is."

"I'll drop by the shed after supper," Dad said.

"Well, he'll do it," Dad said when he came back. "He seemed strangely reluctant, though. It was the extra money that did the trick. He sends most of the money he earns to his relatives in Cambodia. The more money they have, the better off—and safer—they'll be."

Later, after Dad and I had easily put Gary to bed, and Dad had left, I noticed that the vase with the lotus had changed again. It was clear glass now.

"Gary! The vase! Are you changing it on me?"

"Have you ever seen that vase in this house before,

ever?" he said to me. "Anyway, how could I change it, in the wheelchair? You don't know what's happening, do you?" he said with a kind of sly smile.

I wasn't sure I wanted to know. But still I asked. "What's happening?"

"The vase isn't the only thing that's changing. Lisa got more timid. Luke got older and meaner. And my blood got better—the doctor said he had never seen such a dramatic change in blood counts. Mom's different, too. You don't know what all that means?"

I felt cold, even before he said any more. "What . . . what does it mean?"

"Every time we go into the maze we make a huge number of quantum changes. Quantum changes make bifurcations that make new universes—I told you it was proven by this guy Everett. Which means . . . every time we come out of the maze we're coming out into a different universe."

I hardly slept at all that night, worrying. Mainly because the absurd—and terrifying—thing Gary had just told me made absolute sense. And I hated it. I didn't *want* to be in a different universe! I wanted to be home. I felt lost and terrified. Mom was different, Dad was different, Luke and Lisa were different. Were Gary and I different too? I felt like the same person, but was

I? Was that why Gary was getting better? Because every time we left the maze and the universe split, he was a different Gary—a Gary who wasn't as sick as before? There was no way for me to know.

But the house was changing, that was for sure; there weren't the same vases anymore. What else would change the next time we went into the maze? If these were different universes, they were very similar. But what if we hit one that was wildly different? Things were even scarier than I had imagined.

Except for the fact that Gary was getting better. I groaned and rolled over in bed again. I wanted to be at home. But at home Gary would die.

I hated this. Had Gary tricked me? I thought back. When the vase had first changed, he didn't know what it meant, so he hadn't tricked me into another universe then. When had he caught on? Today, had he made us all go in there knowing we would end up in a different universe? Would we ever get back to the original one, our real home, again? Should I just refuse to go along with this anymore?

But he would try to force me—especially if he started getting worse again. And how would *I* feel, if I knew my fear was going to make him die? I stifled another groan. I didn't see what else I could do but go along with him—at least for the time being.

The next morning, I got up when the alarm clock rang at five A.M. I stood behind an apple tree and watched the shed, as Gary had instructed me the night before. A little after six Luke came out of the shed with a canvas bag. I couldn't see everything in it, but the tools seemed to be different from the ones he usually used. There was a saw and the tip of a big hammer. He was also carrying a shovel, as he usually did. Sro-dee was not on his shoulder. As soon as Luke stepped out, he knelt down and reached inside the shed with one hand. I could tell he was saying something, but I couldn't hear what. Then he shut the door firmly and marched off in the direction of the greenhouse. I went to get Gary.

"He left Sro-dee inside, and he didn't lock the door, I'm sure of it," I told Gary after breakfast, as I maneuvered the chair down the ramp. Even though I was stronger, it was harder now, because of the weight Gary had gained. "Why would he leave him inside? He could just let him run around in the garden."

"He left Sro-dee inside because he doesn't want him to follow him to the greenhouse, which is what he'd probably do. That's why I picked it for his new chore."

I felt sorry for Luke for having to work on the horrible, dangerous greenhouse. I also felt sorry for myself for having to go to the horrible, dangerous maze, with only a cat as a guide—and come out into *another* universe. I could hardly believe we were actually going *in* it today, without anybody else standing as a signpost to help us find the way out. "But if we take Sro-dee and get lost inside the maze, Luke will know for sure," I protested. "Gary, I feel lost going into different universes, getting farther from our real home. And maybe—the deeper we go, the more the universe will change."

"Good. What's so great about ours?"

Gary might feel that way, but did I? We had hardly been inside the maze at all so far. All we had seen was the beginning of it. Deeper inside it would be a lot worse. I was thinking I might just refuse to go in.

But then what would Gary do? And what would happen to him? Would he get sicker again? When he was just going to the doctor, he had gotten steadily worse. I was terrified of doing this, but I was also worried about what would happen to Gary if I didn't. And he was right about how I wanted him out of the chair. Sure I wanted my free time back, but I really wanted him to get better. And when he could walk again, he could spend as much time as he wanted in the maze and I wouldn't have to go with him.

But then he'd end up in a different universe from me. Maybe I *couldn't* let him go in alone.

"Okay, so every time we go into the maze we come out into a different universe. But I don't want to be in another universe, I want to go home. And how do we know it's going to be better there?"

"Great-Uncle Arthur made the maze. It's there to do good."

"But what about the things that got worse? Luke, Lisa, both getting more hostile. How do we know we won't end up in a universe where you're sicker?"

"We won't. And Luke and Lisa will get better, too."

How could he be so sure? I parked the chair outside the shed, hoping that Luke had locked the door and I just hadn't seen it. I turned the handle and pushed, and unfortunately it opened. In a heartbeat Sro-dee leapt onto Gary's lap. Gary petted the cat as I began the long march to the woods.

I had slept badly and was drowsy in the morning and hadn't been thinking when I got dressed. Now I realized I was wearing the cutoffs I had seen myself wearing in the maze yesterday, when I had seemed so frightened and we had seemed to be running away from something. Now I knew we would really be going deep into the maze: I had already seen it.

The path tricked us. It ended at the pond.

I felt relief. Gary's shoulders sank, as they had when he had been sicker.

The pond was no longer choked with lotuses. Someone had gone in and cut them down. It could only have been Luke. A pile of withering flowers and leaves and slimy stalks lay on the opposite edge of the water.

But in the water, the lotuses were coming back. They were smaller than they had been, but there were a lot of them. It wouldn't be long before the water would be invisible again. The garden was doing what it wanted, no matter what Luke did to try to stop it.

"Go back," Gary said, his voice hoarse again. "Go all the way back to the meadow and try again. The path *has* to take us there."

"The path does what it wants," I said. But I turned the chair around and went back to the bridge and then on toward the meadow.

Gary bent forward and petted Sro-dee. "Help us, Sro-dee, you beautiful, adorable cat," he said. "Help us get to the maze."

When Gary was well, he would never have talked to a cat like that. He was desperate. I didn't blame him. What would I have done if I were him? Would I dare to make him take me to the maze? Or would I be too afraid of it, and let myself sicken and die, hoping the doctor could help?

I knew we'd get to the maze sometime, because I'd seen myself there in these shorts. But I said to Gary,

"What makes you think this cat will be able to help us get out of there?"

"Because he was Great-Uncle Arthur's cat; he's dead and alive at the same time. Because he's naturally in two different universes. He's a special cat. Aren't you, Sro-dee?" he said, nuzzling him.

We reached the edge of the trees. I pushed the chair out into the sunlight.

We were at the greenhouse. Luke didn't see us at first. He was sweeping broken glass off the cement floor.

I turned the wheelchair around and ran, hoping he hadn't seen us with Sro-dee. I had already done this whole path once and now I was doing it again, running, and Gary was heavier now. Every day this summer was turning out to be a major workout.

Behind us I heard a shout. "Who was that? You have my cat?"

I knew Gary wanted to yell at him that it wasn't really his cat, it was Great-Uncle Arthur's cat, but he was smart enough to keep quiet. I kept running. If Luke was chasing us, he would catch up with us, running freely without the wheelchair. And even though I hoped he would stop us, and keep us from going into the maze, I kept running as hard as I could.

"Hey! Stop!"

Luke's voice was surprisingly still far behind us. I

would have expected him to have caught up with me by now. I ran over the bridge. Where was the path going to end up this time?

"Don't go in there! I will not let you!"

He was gaining on us a little, from the sound of it, but not nearly as much as I would have expected. Was this another trick of the path? What did it want? What was it trying to do?

And by now we could see that we weren't going to the pond. The path only seemed to go to two places in this direction; the pond and the maze. Dread rose up in me, but I kept running. Gary was holding Sro-dee tightly, leaning forward eagerly. "You're gonna make it. I think you're gonna make it," he said, his voice not hoarse anymore, his shoulders not slumping.

"Stop now! Do not go in there!"

His voice was closer, but we had reached the double hedge entrance. "Don't follow us! Don't come in!" Gary screamed at Luke. But I could still sense Luke right behind.

Unlike before, I ran in without hesitation. My hands doubled, then tripled on the wheelchair handles as the process of becoming a probability cloud began.

"Turn left again," Gary said at the T intersection, just as I felt Luke grabbing for my shoulder. I swung the chair around and ran even faster.

The gravel paths between the hedges branched out in a completely senseless pattern. Was it a trick of the path, or were the hedges actually moving, writhing like snakes? I didn't think, I just ran. But for a second I looked to the left and saw a smaller cloud of Gary and myself and the chair. Was that us yesterday? Was I going to see the future again?

A cloud of Lukes ran past ahead of us, not seeing us. Another one ran past us in another direction. Sro-dee was standing up on Gary's legs, alert. But he seemed to have no inclination to jump off. Different colored flowers popped out of the hedges, then disappeared. A cloud of Lukes with huge scissors crossed an intersection far ahead.

"I've got to stop!" I gasped. "I can't keep going like this without a rest."

"Stop," Gary said. "It's too late for Luke to interfere now."

I gradually slowed the wheelchair down, the tires crunching on the gravel. We were at a kind of star intersection, where several paths converged. Amazingly, there was a cloud of stone benches here. I touched it tentatively. As strange as it looked, it felt solid enough. I sank down on it, gasping.

"Good going, Susan," Gary said. He was sitting up straight, his cheeks glowing, holding Sro-dee lightly.

"Sro-dee likes it in here, I can tell. So do I."

The flowers kept growing out of the hedges, then wilting and falling off, like a speeded-up movie. Little piles of wilted blossoms lay on the edges of the paths. Were there five paths converging here, or four? Somehow I couldn't tell—or else it kept changing.

"Do you have *any* idea where we are? Which way to get out of here? Were you watching?" I asked Gary.

"It doesn't matter if I was watching or not," he said. "Once you come in here, you're lost. That's the whole point. It's like the electron going around the universe before it hits the screen."

"But then . . . how are we going to get out?"

Gary took a leash and collar out of his pocket—we had had a little dog named Rusty until a few years ago and his stuff had never gotten thrown away. Gary must have found it in a box somewhere. He carefully put the collar around Sro-dee's neck, and the cat made no protest. "The worst problem is how is *Luke* going to get out," Gary said. "I told him not to come in here. If he could ever find us he could come out with us, with Sro-dee guiding us, but I don't know how he can ever find us."

Gary was still sitting up straight. He looked stronger than I had seen him in months. "Oh, it feels great in here," he said, and then he shouted wordlessly, in exultation.

It was amazing how two people could feel so differently about a place. I was getting my breath back, but I wasn't any more comfortable in here than before. This place was the depth of uncertainty all right, and I hated it. The path being uncertain was bad enough, but in here, *all* the paths were uncertain.

Gary leaned forward, rising up, pointing. "There!" he said. "Look over there!"

I looked where he was pointing. And there on a distant path was a deep probability cloud of Garys, too many to count, blurry and vague and almost transparent. Gary, taller and stronger, walking on his own.

"It's going to work! I knew it was going to work!" he said. "If only Luke could see that, he'd understand. How are we ever going to get him out of here?"

"Maybe Sro-dee could find Luke, and then the way out," I said.

"If he could understand that much."

"Well, I want to get out of here," I said. "It's too creepy being a probability. I don't like not being in one place exactly, even though I'm still so close to myself."

"Well I don't want to get out of here yet, Suze," Gary said. "I haven't felt this strong in months." And even though it was hard to bring him into focus, I could see that he was right. He looked better than ever.

"In fact . . . ," Gary said. He handed Sro-dee to me, who, oddly enough, didn't seem scared at all. Then he began pushing up on the handles of the wheelchair.

"What are you trying to do?" I asked him. "Be careful. If you fall, I don't know if I can pick you up."

"I am being careful," he said. His arms were shaking on the handles, but he was standing. He let go of the handles and remained standing, unassisted. He didn't try to take a step. He must have been able to feel that he wasn't ready for that. But it was amazing how much progress he was making.

Why did it have to be in this horrible place, that kept taking us away from home? And how were we going to find Luke? We couldn't just leave him in here. How big was the maze anyway? There had to be a limit to it, in the real physical world. But were we even *in* the real physical world anymore? If we were in a place of probabilities and uncertainties and discontinuities, a place that took us to a different universe every time we left it, the maze might go on forever.

Gary was looking in another direction, still standing. "Luke! Over here!" he shouted, waving.

I looked where Gary was waving and there was Luke. He saw us. He started toward us. And then the path he was on took a sudden turn and he was out of sight again.

Gary sighed and sank down into his chair. "Why did he have to come in here? The chance of us actually meeting up with him is incredibly low."

I was crying. All I wanted was to get out of here, and maybe Sro-dee *could* help us find the way, for all the reasons Gary had said. But we couldn't leave Luke in here with no way of getting out, we just couldn't. This was the worst catastrophe I'd ever been in. The only part that wasn't horrible was the way Gary was getting so much better, so fast.

"Stand up on the bench and look around, Susan. Hold Sro-dee up so he can see. Maybe there's a chance we can see Luke again and he'll find his way here. We shouldn't move from this spot until we find him."

I stood up on the bench with the cat, feeling hopeless. The hedges were taller than me, but on the bench I could see over them. "Luke! Luke!" I called out, turning around in all directions. Gary started calling, too. If this were a normal place, he might be able to find us by following our voices. But it wasn't a normal place. In the distance I saw a cloud of Susans and Garys in the wheelchair. I also saw a cloud of Garys walking. But I didn't see Luke.

And then a cloud of Lukes stepped from around a corner. We all jerked in surprise. Then Luke's face darkened on the whole cloud. "I told you not to come in here. And why you steal my cat?"

"Oh, Luke, we're so lucky you found us!" I cried out, jumping down from the bench. "Now we can try to get out of here!

"One thing for crazy kids to come to this place. Another to bring my cat. Why you put leash on him?"

Gary didn't answer directly. He simply stood up again. It seemed easier for him this time. Luke's mouth dropped open.

"*That's* why we come in here," Gary said. "Every time we come here I get better. And you must have seen versions of me walking around. Don't tell me you didn't. We saw them. Someday it will take us to that place. That's why we have to keep coming here."

Luke looked away. "Yes, I see. And I see you standing now, for real. If I don't see, I don't believe."

"And we brought Sro-dee because he's a special cat, a scientific cat. If anyone can find the way out of here, it's him. I want to see if it works. Luke, take him on the leash and see where he goes."

"But . . ."

"What else can we do? We can't find our way out on our own. If he can find the way out, then someday I'll be healthy again, like before."

Luke took the Sro-dees and put them on the ground, holding onto the leash. The blur of cats pawed at the gravel and sniffed the ground. Then they started off behind the benches I was sitting on. I jumped up and pushed Gary after the cats.

The cats didn't seem too sure of themselves. They kept stopping to sniff the ground. And at different intersections they stopped and waited, as if trying to make a decision. Now we occasionally saw different versions of ourselves following Sro-dee on other paths. Were they us today? Were they the future?

But now the cats seemed more sure of themselves. They trotted along steadily, not hesitating at the turns. And I knew we were going the right way, because the cloud of us was getting smaller, more solid, less diffuse.

And then we turned a corner and there was the exit, to the left, not the right, as I had somehow expected. Luke took the leash off Sro-dee, threw it in Gary's lap, and scooped up the cat and ran. I ran after him.

The wheelchair was easier to push. I looked down at Gary. He was slumping again. He seemed to have lost weight. My heart skipped a beat.

When we got to the bridge, we slowed down to a more leisurely pace. "Listen, Luke," Gary said. "Do you really feel like working on the greenhouse?"

Luke frowned. "I hate it. I am gardener, not carpenter."

"Well, maybe I can get Dad to change his mind about

it and let you go back to what you like doing. On one condition."

Luke furrowed his brows suspiciously. "Was it your idea he ask me to work on greenhouse?"

"That's not the point," Gary said, avoiding the issue. "If you let us go into the maze with Sro-dee, so he can show us the way out, I'll tell Dad I don't care about the greenhouse anymore. Is it a deal?"

"Well . . ." Clearly Luke cared about the cat and didn't like him going into a crazy place like the maze.

"You saw how he found the way out. You saw how much stronger I am. If you could just let us take him in there, you could go back to gardening—and you'd be helping me get better. Doesn't that matter to you?"

How could Luke argue with that? But he said, "I don't want anything happen to cat—and you and Susan, too. And . . . old man told me about the maze. If Sro-dee go in there without me, I never see him again."

Luke understood—he understood that every time you went into the maze you left your universe behind. That's why he had insisted on following us when we stole Sro-dee and took him in with us. Now I felt terrible. I hadn't realized that's what it would mean to Luke.

But Gary was so insistent on getting well that he ignored it. "But you *saw* me standing up! Could I ever do that before I came to the maze? Every time we go in there it takes me to a place where I'm better. And you know Sro-dee can find the way out—you saw it. And if you came with us, too, then you wouldn't lose him. Please come. Please don't let me die."

"Well, maybe I think about it," Luke said, holding Sro-dee tightly, and we stepped out onto the meadow. The Luke in this universe was still nice enough to consider doing that for Gary. But as for now, he took Sro-dee back with him to the shed. And as they went in, I distinctly heard the click of the door locking Sro-dee inside.

Gary didn't pay attention. He was talking about Wheeler and Everett, and things I didn't understand, like entanglemen, and unreliable branching universes. His voice was hoarse again, and I could see from the position of his legs that he wouldn't be able to stand. He wasn't doing well in this universe, that was clear. He had been wrong that he could only get better. What did that mean about the place we had ended up in this time? I shivered.

As soon as we entered the orchard and saw what was happening on the lawn, I froze. I couldn't push the wheelchair another inch. Gary's voice dried up in a cough.

We were in a dream and a nightmare at the same time.

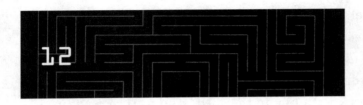

A boisterous cookout rollicked on the lawn behind the house. There was Gary, holding onto a girl, standing straight and strong and throwing his head back in laughter, his arm and chest muscles visible through his polo shirt. And there was I, looking sexy in a short white skirt and sleeveless top, flirting with the handsomest of the older guys. Dad, beaming, turned over the steaks sizzling on the grill, basting them with a wonderful-smelling sauce. Mom was arranging a picnic table loaded with delicious-looking salads and beautiful arrangements of fruits.

And the *current* Gary and I, watching frozen and pale with the wheelchair from the orchard, were the outcasts.

"Let's get out of here, fast, before they—" Gary started to say.

Someone I didn't recognize at first—and then realized was a thinner Lisa with a more fashionable hairdo and pretty clothes—glanced over at us. She frowned, puzzled, and said something to the guy she was talking to.

I turned the wheelchair and ran. It was easier now because *this* Gary was lighter and weaker in *this* universe. I couldn't tell if anyone from the party was following us or not. I pushed on the door of the shed, which of course didn't open. I banged on it. "Luke! Luke! Let us have Sro-dee!" we were both begging him.

There was no answer. Luke didn't know what was happening, he didn't know about the party we had to escape from, and we had no time to tell him. And he didn't want to lose Sro-dee forever.

The voices from the party seemed to be getting closer. Or was I just imagining it? But what if we ran into *ourselves*? That would *have* to be some kind of quantum disaster. We had no choice. I took off for the path.

And once again, the garden seemed to want us not to get caught, because nobody from the party was following us. Or maybe the party was too much fun to go running after some people who might just be Lisa's imagination. I prayed she had been the only one to see us.

"But why . . . ?" I gasped. "Why did we suddenly end up in a universe where both of us already are? You and

I were never here before."

"Just keep going. Just get away from them. If we meet up with ourselves, it will be like matter and anti-matter—we'll wipe ourselves out."

I was sweating, but suddenly I felt cold as we turned onto the path. "We're really going into the maze *without* the cat?"

"Yes, I am." Gary's voice was trembling. Even at his sickest I had never heard his voice tremble like this before. "I'm going in without the cat. And without you, if I have to. But if you know what's good for you, you'll come, too. Otherwise . . . this you and me will never see each other again."

"But how come we were both in that universe and not in the other ones?"

Gary sat up straighter. "Well, the way I figure it is this. Every time we leave the maze, we make a quantum change that splits—bifurcates—the universe, and alters it. But we don't know *when* that change happened. Quantum uncertainty again. The bifurcation could have been one second—or fifty years—or a thousand years—before we left the maze. If it was one second, there would have been no time for things to change a lot and the universe would be almost the same and we'd be the same *us* in it. But I told you about the electron going around the universe. If the bifurcation of the universe happened farther in the past, then more things would have had time to change. The time factor is random—we can't control *when* the bifurcation happens. And maybe the universes with other Garys and Susans in them are universes where we never went into the maze. We're climbing a branching tree of universes. All we can do is keep trying—and hope for the best."

It seemed to me a pretty faint hope. But now at least he could not deny that the maze could make things worse and not just better, as it had at first. It had lured us in and done good things for Gary, but now it was playing tricks like everything else in the garden.

The path was nothing for me to negotiate anymore, especially with Gary being lighter again. "Listen, Gary," I said at the bridge. "If we come out in a place where things are better again—where your blood counts are improving, and where's there are no other versions of you and me—can't we just stay there and *let* things keep getting better? I don't trust the maze, now that it put us in this universe. It could put us someplace even worse."

"We just have to hope."

And then I remembered something Lisa had said, about our parents losing both of us, and I felt my stomach sink. "Gary, the first universe, before we found the maze. We're not there any more, are we? Every time we go inside the maze we leave a universe behind—and leave Mom and Dad there without us? That's . . . that's *horrible*. How can we do that to them?"

"I'm not sure it works that way. We might still be in all the other universes, too. You just *saw* us in this one." But he didn't sound so sure of himself about our being in all the universes. "The books don't agree about that." He sounded like he was just trying to keep me from feeling guilty and refusing to take him into the maze again.

But this time I knew we had to go, even without Sro-dee. Getting away from the disaster of being at that party and running into ourselves was worth the risk.

The path obliged and took us to the maze, not the pond, which was a good thing since even though pushing the chair was easier now, I didn't feel like going all the way back to the meadow again—and risking running into somebody.

We went in—without Sro-dee.

As we became a cloud, I wondered if there were any directions that led to good outcomes rather than bad. But that didn't make sense; the maze didn't know what was good and what was bad in the outside world. Would going deeper make the changes bigger? Maybe. But there was just as much chance of the bigger changes being bad as being good.

But since Great-Uncle Arthur had made the maze, maybe he had put something in it that *would* lead to a good outcome. If he could make the maze at all, then why couldn't he do that, too? And why had he even made it if there wasn't a way to make it take you to a better universe? But how could we ever figure out which was the right way to go to get there?

"I still always feel stronger in here. And you saw me stand up and you saw me walking. That's the universe we have to find."

"But how?"

Gary shrugged. And once again his shoulders didn't seem so thin. "If only Great-Uncle Arthur was around to ask. The books don't tell me. The books don't know about the maze. Only Great-Uncle Arthur did."

After about fifteen minutes, when we were as deep in the maze as we had ever been, and nearly transparent, Gary said, "Okay, let's try to find the way out of here."

I was at a complete loss, without the cat to follow. "But . . . *how?*"

"All I can think of is, keep an eye on the probability clouds. If they seem to be getting smaller, keep going in that direction."

It seemed completely hopeless, but what else could I do? I pushed the wheelchair, turning it this way and that, keeping my eyes on my multiple hands, hoping to see them grow fewer. Sometimes Gary seemed heavier, sometimes he seemed lighter. I went in the heavier direction, hoping it would coincide with the lessening of the probability cloud. And then—miraculously—it did. As Gary sat up straighter, we began to blend together into a more compact bundle. We were approaching the T intersection sooner than I'd expected.

"Well, let's hope for the best," Gary said again, as I turned him toward the exit.

I put my hand to my mouth and started to cry.

The two parallel entrance hedges didn't lead to the path, they led to the pond. A teenage boy was wading into the pond, a boy who looked something like Dad. But we knew it wasn't Dad, because the clothes he was wearing were too old-fashioned even for when Dad was a kid. And as we watched, he bent over and pulled something limp out of the water—the body of a little girl. Aunt Caroline. She was very pale, and beginning to bloat. And still he held her to him, her little head on his shoulder, and swayed back and forth, as if comforting her, tears running down his cheeks.

"Shut up!" Gary whispered to me, and I finally managed to stop crying. Gary gulped. "Oh, wow, this bifurcation happened a long, long time ago," he said in a faint voice.

Then he took control. "Turn around, back to the T. And then just come straight out again and see what we find. The changes seemed less from the original universe when we did that."

Now I was shivering so much I could barely control the chair. But I managed to turn away from this terrible scene and went back to the T intersection, which looked almost friendly in comparison. I squeezed my eyes shut and took a deep breath and turned the chair back around again.

And there was the path and the woods, looking just as they always had. Gary and I both whooped for joy, and then I ran. I wanted to get out there while it was still normal.

We were both jubilant at first, after our close escape, as I hurried along the path. Everything seemed the same. Was it possible we had found a universe very much like our own original one? A universe in which Gary might get better?

The first bad sign was that he wasn't strong, like he had been the day we went to the doctor. If anything, he looked worse than he had when we'd come out that morning with Luke. That was the most important thing, and it hadn't worked this time. Had everything else gotten worse, or were some things better? Could it be mixed at times?

What was Great-Uncle Arthur's secret? And for the first time I wondered if he had left any records. If he had, we had a chance.

Praying we would not run into ourselves, I pushed Garry effortlessly up the ramp to the back porch and into the kitchen. Mom was putting away groceries. She didn't seem surprised to see us the way we were, which was a good sign. On the other hand, she was wearing a different, less flattering outfit than she'd had on that morning, a too-short denim skirt instead of slacks. She also was behaving in an uncharacteristic way, irritably shutting cupboard doors. "Why did you two go out again? Twice a day for a long walk is too much. Gary looks worse. I hold you responsible, Susan."

Gary and I looked at each other. This wasn't the Mom we knew.

She put a jar of smooth peanut butter into a cabinet—always before she had bought chunky—and slammed the door. "We're going to get him onto his bed right now," she said.

Usually she let me take care of that, by myself, or with Dad. "I can do it myself," I said.

"No back talk," she said. "Come on."

This universe was definitely worse than the last one, except that there didn't seem to be any other versions of us, thank heaven. I couldn't wait until we were alone, to discuss it with Gary. And Mom actually made it *harder* to get him onto his bed. I could see him wince when she pulled at his leg.

"Susan, go talk to your friends on your computer or go out or something," Mom said. "Let Gary have his rest before dinner."

"I want to talk to her, Mom. Alone," Gary said.

I could tell that if he hadn't been sick, this Mom would have gotten mad at him. But even in this lousy universe, Mom wouldn't talk that way to her sick son. "All right, but only for a few minutes," she said, and went back into the house.

I sat down on the chair next to the bed. "Wow," I whispered.

"Yeah, we've got to get out of here," Gary said. "But we have to wait until tomorrow. I'm too tired to do it again, and anyway, this Mom wouldn't let us. We have to get through whatever's going to happen here tonight."

"Yeah. Tonight's gonna be a real nightmare. I wish I didn't have to be here."

"Well, you can't go out. I actually feel worse now." He sighed, and then coughed. "At first the universes were getting better. Now they're getting worse. Why did Great-Uncle Arthur do this? Why didn't he put in some way of controlling it?"

"It's quantum. That means unpredictable, you always said," I reminded him.

"Yeah, but there must be a secret to it—a secret way to find a *good* universe, or why make the maze? That's what happened to them all, of course."

"You mean our relatives? They didn't just disappear into nursing homes and die?"

"With no funerals? That's not how it works, Suze. They went into a better universe." He paused, thinking. "And I'm sure Dad knows that's what happened. Okay, Aunt Caroline drowned." He paused. "That was . . . so creepy. Seeing the kid—Dad's father—find her body."

I nodded, feeling terrified all over again.

He went on quickly. "But the other relatives all just disappeared. Dad must have wondered. He must have found out. If he's in a better mood than Mom, we'll have to ask him."

"That won't put him in a good mood," I protested.

"I'll do it," Gary said. "He won't dare get mad at me. But right now I need to sleep. I feel pretty bad. I'll need all the strength I have to get through this."

There was no attic in this house, but there was a basement where a lot of old stuff was stored. I spent the rest of the afternoon down there in the coolness, going through boxes of old papers. And in fact there *were* notebooks, with weird equations in them written in pencil. I had no idea what they meant, the symbols were so strange. I collected them to show to Gary when he woke up, and put them on his porch, with a note that said I had found them in the basement and there might be an answer here somewhere. Gary was right: Quantum was uncontrollable and unpredictable. But if Great-Uncle Arthur had built the maze at all, he must have known something about quantum that other people didn't know—maybe a way of harnessing it to your advantage.

Meanwhile, we had to spend a night in this horrible universe.

Then Mom called for me. She changed her mind about me using the computer or going to visit somebody; I had to help her cook dinner. She was making macaroni and cheese, but here she was using something called "processed cheese food" instead of real cheese the way she used to. It was easier; it was already sort of liquid so you didn't have to grate it. I was sure it wouldn't taste as good. And I was already so sick of the *good* macaroni and cheese she used to make in the original universe. I was sure Gary's appetite for this junk would be very small.

When Dad got home, his first question, as usual, was "How's Gary?" as he put his briefcase away in the front hall closet. Mom was still in the kitchen.

"He's resting," I said, and then added, without thinking, "The maze didn't make him better this time."

Dad's face went white. "The maze? You found the *maze*?"

"Not on purpose," I said quickly. In one way I had made a terrible mistake. But maybe I would learn something. "One day the path just went there, instead of to the pond. You know we've always seen the maze from the bathroom window."

He sank down onto an old couch in the living room. "But you never went in it, did you? No, no, of course not," he said, almost to himself. "That place is dangerous—*really* dangerous." He looked at me hard. "Do you understand?"

I just nodded, not knowing what to say.

"Remember once you asked me if anything else bad happened in the garden, besides Aunt Caroline drowning?" he said.

"Yes, I do remember," I said. "And you kind of avoided it," I dared to add.

"I didn't want to give you any ideas about the maze." He shook his head at me and then leaned forward. "Susan, people go in there and never come out. Did you ever wonder why you have no living relatives except your mother and me?"

"Well . . . yeah." This universe stunk in a lot of ways, but at least he was telling me something he had never told me in another one. That was amazing. It proved that the universes *could* be mixed, bad and good together.

"Because my parents and Uncle Arthur went into the maze. And disappeared. *That* sure took some explaining. Good thing I have my corporate travel agent and my man at the coroner's office. We had to say they all died overseas." He put his forehead in his hand, then looked up at me again. "You say the *path* took you there? How is that possible? The only path in the woods goes to the pond."

"It's a quantum garden, Dad. You must know that."

I waited for him to respond. He just looked at me, his mouth a hard line. As usual, he would admit nothing about the garden. So I just went on.

"The garden was calm for a while but when Gary got sick that triggered the quantum part—quantum and illness are alike in a lot of ways, uncertain, unpredictable. And now the garden's getting weirder and weirder. It all started with the lotuses and the poppies, and then that quantum bird on the screened porch that morning. You and Mom saw it happen."

"Quantum bird? What quantum bird?" He turned to Mom, who had come into the room. "Do you remember anything like that?"

She shook her head. "Susan's been weird all afternoon. I don't know what's gotten into her. And she wore Gary out to a frazzle—she kept him out much later than she should have."

"You must have dreamed it," Dad said to me. "A quantum bird! And you must have somehow gotten lost in the woods and stumbled onto the maze. Paths don't move."

"I . . . I guess you must be right." There was no point in arguing with him now.

"Whatever you do, do not go back to the maze," he told me. "Don't go anywhere near it. It could be the most dangerous place on earth."

I nodded at him obediently. But I was lying. We had to get out of here first thing in the morning.

But what if the next one was worse? Dad's father finding Aunt Caroline's body today was more terrible than anything I could have imagined seeing. I hoped so much that Gary would be able to understand those notes and equations from the basement.

But when I went with Dad to get Gary for dinner, he shook his head at me when Dad wasn't looking. I knew what that meant: There was nothing in the notebooks that would help.

The macaroni and cheese was lousy, and Gary and I

both knew it, but Mom and Dad seemed to think it was the same as always. Gary hardly ate any and Mom fussed at him and he snapped back at her. It was miserable.

So it was a relief when the tentative knock came at the back door. I knew it would be Luke—no one else would knock at the back door. I hopped up and stepped out onto the back porch. "Oh, I'm sorry to disturb you," he said, Sro-dee perched on his shoulder. "I think you are finished eating by now."

"No. Come in," I said.

"No. Better not." He put a yellowed, folded piece of paper into my hand. "Don't show to parent, only to Gary. Very important. From old man. I save it for many years. Maybe it can help you. I go now."

After Dad and I had put Gary to bed and Dad had left, Gary said, "That math is way too far ahead of anything I can understand. Yeah, the answer may be in these notebooks, but I'm not going to be able to figure it out. And if you took it to some professor at a university, that would give the whole thing away and we'd be stuck here."

"Wait. Luke gave me this." I took the folded piece of paper out of my cutoffs pocket.

It was written in a different handwriting from the scrawl in the notebooks, neater and more precise.. "If you are ever truly, truly desperate and need to get away, follow the cat into the maze. Go *only* where the cat leads you, nowhere else. And then follow it out."

Gary and I looked at each other. "I could kick myself for not thinking of it!" Gary said. "I already knew Sro-dee is Schrödinger's cat. Alive and dead at the same time. In more than one universe at the same time. If anything in the world would know how to take the path in the maze that would get to the right universe, the *good* universe, the cat would be it. We've been letting him show us where to go when we leave the maze, but not when we first go in. We've been leading the way instead of following him. That's been our mistake all along." Gary's face brightened. He looked better already.

"And it sounds like Luke decided to let us take Sro-dee, after all," I said, feeling hopeful myself. "Why else would he give us that note? Maybe he'll even come with us, so he won't lose Sro-dee. Tomorrow we go, first thing."

I was awakened in the middle of the night by a flashing light outside my window. I ran downstairs. It was an ambulance. While Mom and Dad hovered, two men were carrying Gary out in a stretcher. A nurse held an IV bottle over his head and there was a breathing tube going into his nose. Gary feebly beckoned to me and I leaned over him, my ear next to his mouth.

"Go," he managed to whisper. "Go tomorrow and follow the cat into the maze, while there's still a chance."

"Without you?"

"I might not make it in this universe. You have to find the one where I do."

The ambulance screamed off into the night.

I cried and cried as I lay in bed, not hoping to sleep. This was it. I would never see Gary again—*my* Gary, the one I had grown up with. He was probably going to die. And even if by some miracle he didn't, I had to go into the maze again, and the Gary I would find in whatever universe I ended up in—even if it was a good one—would be different. *How* different would depend on when the bifurcation happened.

Despite everything I had gone through, how hard we had both tried, I had lost Gary forever. I kept on crying.

I tried to focus on tomorrow, and doing what Gary had asked. I was going to have to go in alone. And I would have only Sro-dee to depend on, if Luke would really let me take him away forever. But why else had he given me the note?

Did I dare to hope Luke might come with me? Somehow, I doubted it.

As I lay there unsleeping, the more I thought about the note, the more worried I got. It didn't make sense. If our relatives had found the right universe by following Sro-dee, then why was Sro-dee here, and not with them?

Maybe they hadn't had to follow Sro-dee, because Great-Uncle Arthur had built the maze and knew its secrets. Maybe he had left Sro-dee here as a kind of escape device for Luke, whom he seemed to have liked. After all, he had shown him the maze. Maybe Luke wasn't completely safe and legal, as Dad claimed, and Great-Uncle Arthur knew it. Luke and the cat sure seemed attached to each other.

Or maybe Great-Uncle Arthur had left the cat in case some terrible thing happened, like with Gary. The garden had become quantumly active only after Gary had gotten sick. Gary's illness must have triggered the quantum phenomena, as I told Dad. Was that the way Great-Uncle Arthur had set it all up?

That thought made me more hopeful. Maybe I *hadn't* lost Gary after all. Maybe the Gary who had gone to the hospital wasn't the original one—he was so much sicker. The Gary from before had been getting better. And

I has seen him walking in the maze ahead of me on his own, looking perfectly healthy. *That* was the Gary I had to go into the maze to find.

I had just managed to get to sleep when the front door opening woke me up. I went right down.

It was Dad. He looked ashen. "Well?" I said.

He looked at me silently for a moment, as if he was too miserable even to answer my question. Then he took a handkerchief out of his jacket pocket and wiped his forehead. "They had to put him on a real respirator, not just an oxygen tube in your nose like in the ambulance. It goes into your mouth and makes your lungs work. You have to be sedated or your reflexes would fight it. You can only be on it for a few days or your lungs will be irreparably damaged. If he can't start breathing on his own before then, well, then . . ." He couldn't finish, but he didn't have to. "Your mother stayed with him."

Dad hugged me.

I had to go into the maze as soon as possible and get to a universe where Gary was better. That had been his final request to me and I would never forget the words: "I might not make it in this universe. You have to find one where I do."

But it was still dark out and I couldn't go if I couldn't see. And I was going to have to act normal, eat breakfast, all that, so Dad wouldn't get suspicious, now that he knew I knew about the maze. I helped him upstairs, then went back to my room. And I was so exhausted that I slept, despite everything. Dad had to wake me for breakfast.

We didn't eat much. I had to wash up because Dad was going straight to the hospital to help them. "There's no point in you coming yet, Susan," Dad said. "He's unconscious. When he starts breathing on his own again and wakes up, we'll come and get you. They said it wouldn't be long." But I could tell by the way he said it that he didn't believe it. With illness, as with quantum, you never knew.

When Dad had left and the dishes were done, I went to the shed. I could smell incense even from outside, so I knew Luke was up—maybe he was praying for Gary. He must have heard the ambulance and known what it meant. And if he didn't know that this Gary was worse than ever, in the hospital, then he needed to know, so he *could* pray for him. I wasn't sure prayer would do any good, but anything was worth a try. I knocked at his door.

In a moment the lock clicked and the door opened. "Hello, Susan," Luke said, his face looking heavy and lined. "I am very sorry about Gary."

"You heard the ambulance? You know he's in the hospital? On a breathing machine." I gulped back a sob and wiped the tears out of my eyes.

"I know he is in hospital. I pray as much as I can."

Sro-dee rubbed against my ankle and I petted him. That was a good sign. Gary was always the one who had interested the cat before; he had never paid much attention to me. If Luke let me take him, it seemed like the cat was willing to guide me.

"Do you know . . . what I have to do?" I asked Luke. "You must have read the note a hundred times."

"I know you have to follow Sro-dee, so he can take you to the place where Gary will live. I have to say good-bye to Sro-dee forever now. He will not be coming back to this place."

"Maybe you don't have to lose him!" I said, begging him. "Maybe you could come, too."

"No. Not for me to go to that place, even though the old man give me that note. Lord Buddha says we must not want anything. If I go to an unholy place like that again, just so I can keep this cat, it would not be right."

I couldn't argue with Luke's religious beliefs; they were obviously very strong. "Will you miss Sro-dee? Or will you forget that you ever had him?"

"Better if I could forget. But I didn't forget the old man when he went to whatever place he went to. So I don't think I will forget the cat." He sighed. "But cat is getting very old. This is last thing he has to do. Most important thing." He picked Sro-dee up and held him against his shoulder for a long moment, stroking him. "Okay. Bye-bye now. You take good care of Susan. Help her." Then he said something I didn't understand, which had to be Cambodian. He must have thought the cat would understand it better. I hoped so. I had never believed animals understood what people said to them. Now I wished I did.

He handed me the cat and stood and looked after us as I carried him through the garden. There were more weeds than ever now, and everything was unkempt. Luke must have been praying more than weeding. I had always hated the garden, but now, strangely, I felt sad to see it in such bad shape.

I was going into teh maze *alone*, with only the cat. I almost hoped the path would take me to the pond, but I couldn't hope that. I had to get to the universe where Gary was well. We knew there was one. We had seen him walking in the maze. We had seen him at the party.

Would *we* ever be the Gary and Susan at that party?

The path went right to the maze. It was so fast without the wheelchair—too fast. I wanted to put if off. But I couldn't. I had to do what Gary had asked.

I put Sro-dee down, holding lightly onto the leash. At first he just stood there, not even going to the T intersection. Then he began to walk, very slowly, like the times he had taken us back, as though he were feeling for the right way.

It was a warm day but I was shivering again, I was so afraid. Sro-dee hesitated at the T intersection, then turned right. Then everything was completely confusing and I entirely lost track of where we were going. It was all the same—the tall hedge, the flowers coming out of it, the wilted petals at its base, the twists, the turns, the branchings. The sky was full of scudding clouds, so it was shadowy in here. I kept looking for a group of Garys walking, hoping that's how it would work and I could just go back with him. But, unlike those other times, I saw no one else in the maze.

And now I could barely see Sro-dee, or myself. We had spread out into such huge probability clouds that we were transparent, nearly invisible. Did that mean we were going to a universe that was very, very far away, where everything would be totally different?

I pushed that thought from my mind. It didn't bear thinking about. And if the note was right, the cat would never take me to a place like that.

I wanted the old universe, with Gary always off playing sports and ignoring me, and me going to high school next year. But in all the times we had been in the maze, the probabilities had never become so many. If I hadn't had the leash, I wouldn't have been able to follow Sro-dee. He seemed to be everywhere at once, on many different paths. How long was this going to go on? When were we going to get solid again? I was thinking I couldn't stand this for another minute. But what choice did I have? I couldn't just leave the cat and try to get back on my own. Then I'd be in an even worse mess.

But just when I was about to reach the breaking point and start screaming for help—as if there were anybody to hear me—I noticed that Sro-dee began to look more solid. We had taken a specific path, the path the cat wanted to take. And soon I would find out what kind of universe he had taken me to.

The note to follow the cat had been meant for Luke. Maybe it would be a universe that would be right for him, but not for Gary and me.

We reached the T intersection. There was the path and the woods, thank God. I picked up Sro-dee as we walked between the last two hedges and became solid again.

The first thing I noticed was the difference in the path. It was much better cared for than the path in the other universes. It was sharp-edged, and very smooth and flat, and there were no twigs or roots on it. It was scary.

And it got scarier. When we emerged into the mead-

ow, the wildflowers were so abundant you could barely see the grass underneath them. When we passed by
the valley, there were more pink and blue phlox than I
had ever seen, and they were bigger, some blossoms
almost a foot across. The shrubs in the long avenue
were taller than me and absolutely engulfed in blossoms, and there was not a weed to be seen.

This was not the old universe. This was somewhere
beautiful, but very different. Maybe it had been a huge
mistake to follow the note meant for Luke.

I stopped and gasped when we reached the shed.
There was an addition to it, also made out of stone,
with more windows. The hill to the outhouse had neat
rows of flowers, perfectly trimmed and weeded. Maybe
it was my imagination, but the apple trees seemed
taller.

The lawn behind the house looked like a lawn in some
fancy public garden, the kind of lawn you weren't supposed to walk on, manicured and lush at the same time,
and the deepest green I had ever seen.

Three elderly people sat chatting in canvas-and-wood
chairs around a table on the lawn, one woman and two
men. There was something vaguely familiar about
them. I hardly dared to approach them. Did our family
even live here any more?

Then one of the old men, the bald one with the goatee, saw me. He gestured to the others. They all stopped talking and just turned and stared at Sro-dee and me.

I took one more step toward them, then stopped.

The other man, who had a full head of white hair, beckoned. "Come. No need to be afraid. We know Sro-dee well. You can only have come from the maze. You must be our relative."

I stepped closer, tentatively. "But . . . do you live here? This was always our family's house."

"Susan! My granddaughter!" cried the man who had welcomed me. He stood up and hugged me, then sat down again, an expression on his face that was a strange mixture of joy and worry.

"Then you are my grandniece," said the bald man with the goatee. "I am Arthur Strohl, winner of the Lebon Prize. And builder of the maze." There were what looked like old newspaper clippings on the table. "Would you like to see some articles about me?"

Maybe he was a genius, but he sure seemed full of himself. He was so different from his brother, my grandfather. "Er . . . sure, in a minute." I turned to the others. Sro-dee immediately jumped into my grandfather's lap, and the older man fondled him, smiling.

The woman had a long white braid; she didn't seem to care about the cat, and she wasn't smiling. "Are you my grandmother then?" I dared to ask her.

"I am your father's mother, Edith," the woman said. She was my grandmother, but she wasn't warm or welcoming like my grandfather, not the least bit grandmotherly at all. Nor did she seem at all surprised or pleased to see me.

"But . . . I don't get it. This is our family's house and we've always been living in it, every time we came out of the maze."

"But this time you followed the cat into the maze, is that correct?" my grandfather, holding Sro-dee, asked me. He was the only one who seemed interested in me. "Luke must have told you to do that. Something must be going very wrong in your world."

"It's my brother, Gary. He's in the hospital and—"

"Go back to the shed and get a chair," my father's mother, Edith, said. "You need to sit down so we can talk." Her voice was cold. I bet Dad hadn't minded much when *she* disappeared.

I went back to the shed. Just inside the door was a stack of folding chairs. I didn't look around, I didn't *want* to look around, to see if there was another Luke here. I carried one of the old-fashioned chairs back to where they were sitting, unfolded it, and sat down.

"So the disaster that brought you here is your brother's illness?" my grandfather asked. He seemed so much nicer than the other two.

"Before I tell you about it, could you please tell me where I am?" I said. "I know we enter a new universe every time we leave the maze, and they would sometimes be a little bit different, and sometimes horribly different. But my mother and father were always living in this house when we came here before."

"I built the maze for two reasons," Great-Uncle Arthur said. He banged his fists on the wooden armrests of his chair. "It still pains me that I would have won the Lebon again for achieving this, but it had to be a secret, or else the world would have flocked here, and then it wouldn't have worked. One reason was so that our family could come to this world and be safe here forever—safer even than in the original garden."

He paused for a moment, which gave my grandfather a chance to put in, "But your father wouldn't come," he said sadly to me. "He wanted no part of it."

Now I understood why Dad was always so close-mouthed about the garden.

"And because he wouldn't come," my grandfather went on, "I was worried about something just like you describe, like one of you getting dangerously ill, or financial ruin, or a terrible war. I trusted Luke. When Arthur said he could get to this place, and your father wouldn't come, I wanted to leave a way that whoever in our family stayed could follow. The quantum effects must be growing larger in the garden, are they not?"

"Yeah," I said, feeling a little breathless. "Poppies and lotuses growing, and a quantum bird on the porch, and the path moving, taking us to the maze. That's how Gary and I found it. Before we could only see it from the upstairs bathroom window."

"And now Luke has lived up to my expectations and given this universe to you by giving up Sro-dee and letting him take you here. I was the one who gave Luke the note. Things must be very bad indeed with your brother for Luke to do that—and for the garden to go quantum."

My grandmother with the long white braid and the white slacks cleared her throat. "Your grandfather is very kindhearted," she said, with the first hint of warmth I had heard in her voice.

But even though she seemed to be trying to be kind, I didn't feel it was real. I was beginning to dislike her and Great-Uncle Arthur, the bragging prizewinner. I almost wished that my grandfather hadn't married her—except that then I wouldn't exist.

"My brother Gary is dying," I said. "He's sixteen, two years older than me. He's in the hospital, on a respirator. If they don't get him off the respirator as soon as possible, it will destroy his lungs. There . . . there really isn't much hope. I'm trying to find a universe where

Gary will be well."

My grandmother patted a pile of three books on a folding table next to her chair. "These are the books I have written. No publisher was wise enough to understand them, so I had to pay to have them published myself."

What was wrong with these people? My grandfather was the only one who seemed to care about anyone but himself. The other two seemed so self-involved they were almost addled. Maybe that was why my grandfather had come with them and left us behind—they needed looking after.

"What about Caroline?" I asked him, thinking about seeing him find her body.

My grandfather looked away sadly.

Arthur sighed, and then said, "That was the beginning of this idea. I didn't want anything like that to happen again. Here, it couldn't happen." He paused, and put his hand to his chin. "Still, it was probably just as well that poor Caroline didn't live out her full life. She was different from us, almost feebleminded."

These people were *monsters*. Except for my grandfather. Now I knew why Dad had always been so devoted to him. "Please. Please, can anybody help me? I told you about Gary. When Luke gave me the note about following the cat, I thought it might take me to a universe where he would be well again. We *saw* him walking in the maze, after he stopped being able to walk in our own universe. We saw ourselves at a party on this very same lawn. Is there any way we can both be the ones in that place? Why did Luke think coming here would help me?"

"It would have helped Luke to come here," my grandfather said, and his shoulders sagged a little, as if he missed Luke. "This universe is very, very far away from the original one. In this universe, only the garden exists. We are completely self-sufficient. Our workers take care of the garden and grow the food. Luke would have been safe here, with his beloved cat, for a long, long time. I'm . . . I'm sorry about Gary. I do remember him." He sighed. "He was such an active little boy, always running. Of course, it was his illness that triggered the quantum effects in the garden. Illness and quantum have so many similarities—they are both chaotic, both unpredictable, and no one really understands them deeply enough. It was Gary's illness that made the path bring you to the maze. But it didn't help. So sad to think of him dying at sixteen."

I jumped up. "You mean my coming here isn't going to do *anything* to help him? It's just a place for you to hide—and for somebody else if they needed to? And after I went through the maze so far, all by myself!" I turned to Arthur. "You're the one who made it. Isn't there *any* way to control the universe you end up in—except for following the cat and coming to this one?" This universe, where everything was so perfect, and everybody but my grandfather was so heartless and self-involved.

And then I realized that when Luke talked about "the old man" he had meant my grandfather, and *not* Great-Uncle Arthur, as I had always assumed.

"The maze is a discontinuity. You must have some understanding of that if you have been in it several times," Arthur said. "My miraculous invention was to make a way that would unfailingly come here, to this world, that I could find. The disaster equation. Schrödinger's cat inherently understands it. I had to follow that equation in order for us to get here—an equation someone *else* may discover some day and get all the credit for." He banged his fist on the chair again, then sighed, and calmed down a little. "But the cat is a discontinuity, too. He is the original Schrödinger's cat. Except for me knowing how to get here with my equation, only the cat can know where he is going. Even *I* have an equation only for this universe. I couldn't tell you how to get to where you want to go."

I couldn't help it; tears ran down my face. My grandmother looked away from this unseemly display of emotion.

I sniffed, and got a piece of tissue I luckily had in my pocket, and wiped my eyes and blew my nose. I turned back to my grandfather, who was holding Sro-dee.

He was petting the cat, and whispering to him. Yeah, it was great that he and the cat got along and they were together again. And maybe the cat understood the maze, and how to get to *this* boring universe. But cats didn't understand human language. What was my grandfather thinking of, whispering to him like that?

Okay, Arthur didn't have the answer. But was it possible my grandfather had one? Sro-dee was purring in his lap, even more intensely than he purred with Luke. And Grandpa—I felt I could call him that—was still talking to him. I couldn't hear what he was saying. Was it even English?

I suddenly just had to get to a universe where Gary *was*, I had to see him again, ill or well.

Grandpa looked up at Arthur. "Write down the equation, Arthur," he said. "And not in your usual scribble. Make it legible."

"The equation?"

"Yes!" Grandpa said irritably. "The disaster equation you were just talking about that beats the maze and invariably takes you here. Just write it down."

"Who are you to give me orders? I won the Lebon

Prize."

"Do you want to be stuck with a teenager here forever? You know she will never get any older."

"No. But I don't see what—"

"Just write it. And give me a blank piece of paper, too."

Arthur took a pencil out of his shirt pocket, one of those old-fashioned ones that never needs sharpening because you put pieces of lead in it. He had a little notebook in his pocket, too. He put the notebook on the table and on it he painstakingly wrote something out that went all the way across the page. He tore the page off and handed it to Grandpa, along with another piece.

"Do you have your compact handy, dear?" Grandpa asked Edith. I had noticed that she was very carefully made up.

"What do *you* want my compact for?" she said.

Again he asked, "Do *you* want to be stuck with a teenager here forever?"

She opened her old-fashioned white leather purse and handed him a compact. He put it on the table. He held Arthur's equation over the compact and very carefully wrote the reflection of it down on the blank sheet of paper.

Still holding Sro-dee, he took a wallet out of his pocket and got a safety pin out of it. "Never know when you'll need one of these," he said. He carefully pinned the reflection of Arthur's equation to Sro-dee's collar.

"You're right, Arthur. Sro-dee is a special cat, even more special than you know." Grandpa turned to me. "You are a brave girl, to risk coming here. Now you have to be brave again. I am hoping that if you follow Sro-dee again, the reversed equation will take you back to the world we came from—your original world. Gary may be sick there. But he also may not be. It has been years since we left—years of continuous quantum changes at tiny levels, making bifurcations at our levels. Things may be different there now, after your passage through the maze. But I think it is your only hope."

He stood up and I stood up. "I am very happy to see that you have become such a brave and caring young woman. I wish you all the luck I can." He caressed Sro-dee a last time and handed him to me.

"She turned out good-looking enough, anyway," Grandma Edith said, without getting up.

Arthur didn't get up either—I wasn't important enough. "I'm the scientist in the family, not just a gardener. God only knows where you'll end up or if it will be remotely like where you came from. It could be very unpleasant. You'd be safer just staying here, but there isn't any room."

No room! There was plenty of room. They were just too selfish to share. Not that I wanted to stay with these people for another minute anyway—except for Grandpa.

"Sro-dee and Luke are very close," Grandpa said. "He might be able to find him. Good luck, Susan." He kissed me on the cheek.

"I'm very glad I got to meet you, Grandpa," I said. "Thanks for trying to help me." I didn't say anything to the others as I walked away.

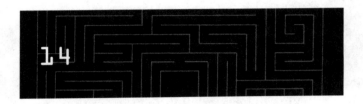

14

When I had left the old garden, I had felt sad that it was so neglected. But this one was worse—it was too perfect. Maybe I wouldn't have felt that way except that Edith and Arthur had been so awful. I was glad they had left our world forever. What would it have been like to grow up with them around?

It was scarier this time because I didn't know if Srodee knew where he was going. The note from Grandpa to Luke had said to follow the cat, and that indicated the cat knew how to get to this universe. But did he know how to get back? The maze was so changeable.

And why had Arthur had to tell me that the maze might go to someplace extremely unpleasant? If I ended up in some nightmare world, what would I do? Nothing but go back into the maze and try again. I might have to spend my whole *life* trying to find the right world.

Again, Sro-dee was very tentative. Again, we spread out into a huge probability cloud. It seemed to go on longer this time. Trying not to groan, I clutched the leash and followed the cats through the twisting, changing pathways. I prayed the reversed equation would work. How many times could I stand going through this?

Freezing snow pelted my face. A sudden blizzard in the middle of June. Huge white flakes gusted down in the wind. It seemed to have been going on for a while, because it was deep on the ground. Sro-dee was having trouble making his way through it.

And then the cats just sat down and began licking their paws, making multiple imprints in the snow. They had never done that before in the maze, they had always just kept going. Now, in the middle of a blizzard, with me desperate to find Gary, the probability cloud of cats had decided to be recalcitrant.

I didn't know what to do. "No! Oh, please no," I cried, shivering. I felt like the cold from the snow was working its way deep inside my body. There had been a lot of bad moments, but this one was the worst.

I had to get the Sro-dees moving—in the direction of the equation pinned to their collars.

All the Susans knelt down and petted the Sro-dees. I

held the equation up directly in front of their eyes. It was getting wet from the snow and beginning to be harder to read. "Luke," I said. "Go back to Luke. Find Luke. This is the way."

The Sro-dees did not respond. My heart sank. Was I stuck here forever? Would I freeze or starve to death? I knew I couldn't take a step that wasn't to follow the cat. If I did I would never get out—or else I'd end up in one of the extremely unpleasant universes that Arthur had been kind enough to mention.

And then the Sro-dees licked the Susans' hands with their rough, warm tongues. It was the most wonderful feeling. The cats stood up and began to move. And in a few minutes the blizzard was gone. Were we possibly going to make it?

Finally we began to solidify. My heart skipped a beat as I picked up Sro-dee and walked between the last two hedges. When we were both completely solid I carefully unpinned the wet piece of paper with the equation on it from Sro-dee's collar and put it in my pocket. We could look in Gary's books and find out what it meant—though I hoped Gary wouldn't be reading all those quantum books anymore.

The path looked normally unkempt, which was a good sign. I prayed it would take me to the right place. The bridge looked the same. Did I dare to hope?

The path went to the meadow. It looked as I had always remembered it. I felt exhausted—even though I was not pushing the wheelchair—but I had to know. I turned around, still holding, and walked all the way back down the path again. It took me to the pond. There were no lotuses.

I felt a surge of hope.

I walked more slowly down the path, which took me safely to the meadow again. Past the valley, also normal. Luke—a younger and sturdier Luke—was weeding in the long avenue. "Hi, Luke," I said, putting Sro-dee down beside him. "I just took Sro-dee for a little walk.

Luke looked up at me with his old grin. "Glad to see you are having a good day today, Susan," he said.

"I think I might be having a *very* good day," I said. Everything seemed normal so far. I just wished I didn't feel so tired.

Luke was weeding, not praying. And there was no ramp on the back porch! That was the best sign of all.

Now I just had to find out about Gary for sure.

I walked into the kitchen. There was a sandwich and a salad on the table—and a pill organizer. "Susan, where have you been?" Mom said, fussing over me, wearing a long skirt. "It's past your lunchtime. I want you to try to eat it all today."

"*My* lunchtime?" I said, totally baffled. "But what

about Gary? Is he off the respirator?"

"Gary? Respirator? I don't know what you're talking about. He's at baseball practice, as usual. Do you want to have your lunch out on the porch? I'll carry it out there for you. You go out there and sit down now in your chair."

"My chair? The porch?" I was completely confused. What was Mom talking about?

"You know what the doctor said. Be a good girl, dear."

She was talking to me like I was a baby. It didn't make sense. "What doctor?" I said.

"Why are you acting so funny, Susan? Don't you remember what he said? Getting over-tired will just make things worse."

That was what they had said to Gary when he had first started getting sick and refused to believe it. "Gary's at baseball practice?" I said. "But . . . what about the wheelchair?"

"What wheelchair?" Now she seemed confused. It was great she didn't know about the wheelchair. Maybe I had found a universe where Gary wasn't sick. But then why was she talking about a doctor?

"Susan, just go out to the porch and have your lunch there. Your special chair's more comfortable. The doctor said you need your nourishment."

The doctor had also said that about Gary when he had first gotten sick. Now I *did* feel sick. A horrible realization was beginning to dawn on me. "Just let me . . . go upstairs first," I said. "I want to get something from my room."

"We already moved everything you wanted out to the porch."

"I'll be right down and I'll rest all afternoon," I said. I *felt* like resting all afternoon.

I dragged myself up the stairs and into the bathroom. I looked out the window, praying.

The maze was still there. I groaned with relief. Gary or Sro-dee might be able to save me. I wanted to do it as soon as possible, while I could still walk. I didn't want Gary pushing me in a chair.

And I didn't feel like eating lunch—the thought of food was sickening. I went quietly back downstairs again. Mom wasn't in the kitchen, and neither was the food—she must be setting it up on the porch. I just felt like collapsing, but I had to get out of here. Gary wasn't here. I had to go find Luke and Sro-dee and *make* them go to the maze with me. I went as fast as I could out the back door.

Gary and the good-looking Lisa were approaching the steps, holding hands. Was he dating her now?

As soon as Gary saw me, he dropped Lisa's hand and

came bounding up the back steps, taller and handsomer and more energetic than ever. I staggered out of his way and almost fell.

"Suze? Where are you going? You should be resting," he said. "I came back during break to see how you were doing."

I had done all this to try to be a good person, to try to help. And look what had happened to me!

"Gary! We've got to get back to the maze. We have to get out of here—to a place where we're *both* well."

"The maze? *That* old story, the optical illusion in the glass upstairs?" He held open the door for me. "I think you better come in and lie down. I hope it's not . . . not getting into your brain now, too."

He led me to the porch, where Mom had left my food and pills. Lisa followed us. Stacked next to my bed were books—physics books—with dozens of bookmarks stuck inside. I didn't resist now as Gary guided me to the bed. I fingered the piece of paper in my pocket, the one with Great-Uncle Arthur's equation on it. As I looked back out at the garden, I saw Sro-dee chasing a butterfly. My brain felt fine.

About the Author

For more than thirty years, William Sleator has thrilled readers with his inventive books, which blend real science with stories that explore our darkest fears and wishes. His *House of Stairs* was a groundbreaking book for young adults, named one of the best novels of the 20th century by the Young Adult Library Services Association. Critics call his writing "clever and engrossing . . . and just plain fun" (*Booklist*) and "gleefully icky" (*Publishers Weekly*).

Mr. Sleator divides his time between homes in Boston, Massachusetts, and rural Thailand.

This book was designed by Jay Colvin and art directed by Becky Terhune. It is set in monotype Apollo. The display type is OCRA.